The Wanderlust (And the Caste of Feathers)

This is a work of fiction. Any names of real persons living or dead are coincidental.

Library of Congress Cataloging-in-Publication Data is available upon request.

ISBN 978-1-7334244-2-4

I lovingly dedicate my work to my family, especially my Mother, for she has loved me unconditionally and has supported me perpetually. I also wish to kindly recognize my many friends, particularly Andrew, for helping me make this dream come true. It has been a distinct pleasure working with you on this publishing project. Finally, affectionately, I devote my story to all the admirers of Anatidae everywhere.

Foreword

Well, it's about time.

That's what I thought when Brian first talked to me about potentially publishing this little story of his. He first wrote it about a quarter century ago. We've been impatiently waiting for him to publish the thing ever since. treamAnd now it seems the time has finally arrived.

I've known Brian since the late 1970's. Yes, we're old, but we were very young then. We were little single digits with big imaginations and aspirations of telling stories just like this one. So like I said at the beginning, it's about time.

If it seems like I'm grumpy, that happens to be Brian's favorite adjective for me. You clearly have a lot in common with him. So this should be right up your alley. Even if you somehow don't think I'm grumpy, you should like this. I'm grumpy, and I like it. It's a sweet little coming-of-age story about an adolescent duck trying to find his way in the world. This means if you don't like, you're probably even more grumpy than me. And that's no way to be.

Drew Sheldon is the author of the trauma-focused memoir "Things I Could Never Tell My Mother (And Some Things She Told Me)" and the upcoming "More Things I Could Never Tell My Mother (And Some Things I Did)".

Chapter 1

Zephyr lightly bent the cattails, a profusion of them, adoring the wide river, flanking each side of it. There was an abundance of towering trees, thereby creating a dense forest, allowing shafts of sunlight to penetrate the landscape. Butterflies, fluttering seemingly aimlessly, danced above the slow, yet steady brown water, while the dragonflies would dart across its surface and the clusters of lily pads.

Indeed, it was idyllic environment for the Colony of Ducks, all of whom had settled there, years ago. The Honored Founders could not have chosen a better place to establish what they called a utopia. Hidden away in isolation, there were thankfully precious little threats to the Colony. And, if something ominous ever approached, the blue jays, with whom the Colony had made an arrangement, based on the sharing seeds, and they would warn the ducks with their strident shrieking. They were excellent sentries.

Sustenance was never a problem, either. The river, and its environs, provided enough for everyone, including the jays, which was the deal that was made with them, in exchange for their watchful services.

Even the weather was kind to the Colony. In the summer, the density of the trees kept the ducks cool from the heat, and afforded them shelter from any copious rainstorms. When it became wintertime, the beavers, also denizens of the river, and apt architects of manipulating wood, would use their skills and build lodges, comprised of rocks, sticks, mud, and twigs, for their feathered friends. Unlike the jays, they wanted nothing in return. Their joy, it

1

seemed, was helping their neighbors, and, of course, the making of dams, which benefited the river, which thereby controlled flooding. The beavers also worked closely with the River Inspectors, those members of the Colony that were responsible for ascertaining the wellbeing of the watercourse.

Was it possible to feel restless, even boredom, in paradise? Evidently, it was for Drazzle.

Drazzle Fairfeather was a young duck. Were he human, he'd be equivalent to a teenager. Similarly to the other ducks, he was as white as a cloud. However, in his feathers, there were distinct tinges of yellow. His bill, an average size, was the color of a wild tiger lily flower, a bright orange. His legs and webbed feet were of the same aforesaid bill color. His tail feathers curled cutely.

He was respectful and very intelligent. In school, he earned good grades, and his teacher, Mister Poom, appreciated his yearning for learning. Among those of his own age, he didn't have any friends, only, at best, acquaintances. And those he had, precious little that they were, had drifted away, due to Drazzle's withdrawal from routine interests. Unfortunately, it was this previously mentioned withdrawal that made him a target for ridicule, and misperception. Some of his classmates thought he was haughty, a paradox for Drazzle, since, despite his academic aptitude, he often felt so unremarkable. A private truth, in fact, which, given what he was feeling, was a puzzle all its own. Aside from Drazzle's peers, the adults in his life thought he was simply going through the awkward stages of ascending adolescence.

Drazzle's best friend, also an adolescent in human terms, was a red cardinal named Zeet Redpebble. Drazzle liked the little red bird because he was spunky, caring, and loyal. Notwithstanding these ideal traits for a confidante,

Drazzle nevertheless distanced himself even away from Zeet. He knew he could tell Zeet anything, but he simply couldn't articulate the words. Zeet, being respectful, gave his friend space, and said he was available to talk, when Drazzle was ever ready.

Drazzle was old enough to think about getting a job, yet none appealed to him. His own father was the Director of the Division of Defense. Getting assigned to the Division would be easy, in fact, a rite of passage, but, right now, nothing felt easy for him.

Drazzle preferred his time alone. However, such a preference wasn't always feasible. Idly, as he sailed down the river, Druful and his buddies appeared from the riverside and entered the water. For all his life, Druful was a bully for Drazzle. Druful was bigger, physically stronger, and, as an unhappy consequence, much louder. Druful was with his usual clique, all comprised of young male ducks their own age.

From behind Drazzle, Druful said, "Hey, look, buddies, its Drazzle, the Daydreamer. Drazzle, the Loner. Drazzle, the Loser!"

They all laughed. It was a rude, taunting sound. Drazzle did his best to ignore it. He was smart enough to know, if he gave in to Druful, it would only motivate him all the more to engage.

Nevertheless, Druful was never the one to relent so simply.

"You think you're too good for us, don't you?" yelled Druful. "Well, unlike you, I'm not wasting any time, no way. I'm gonna be a River Inspector, just like my Dad. I'll be doing something useful, while you mosey down the waterway. You're pathetic!"

More insolent laughter ensued. Drazzle paused and slowly turned his head. He was about to say something to his detractors, when Zeet suddenly flew down from the treetops. Hovering in the air, Zeet took a betwixt stance. The red of his feathers matched his fervor.

"Leave my friend alone!" Zeet shouted.

"Look at this, fellas," Druful began. "Drazzle's not *duck* enough to fight his own battles. He's gotta have a speck of a bird to do it for him!"

Further laughter erupted from Druful and his goons. Zeet was undaunted.

"I'd rather be a speck, instead of a brainless clump of feathers!"

Druful was incensed. He wasn't going to brook an insult from a cardinal.

"C'mon, boys, let's show these wimps who's brainless!"

Momentarily, the other ducks looked at one another with confusion. But, when Druful started to advance, the intent became clear to them, no matter how badly worded it was. However, before the skirmish could proceed, a shriek from above said, "Stop it, all of you!"

The voice of the screech came from a blue jay, which had swooped and landed on a log nearby. It was Blex, a sentry, and a member of the Division of Defense.

"Break this up, or I'll again report you all to your parents!" Blex said, sternly.

Druful said something unkind under his breath and departed. The others followed.

Blex looked at Drazzle and Zeet. "Am I going to have any additional trouble from you two?"

"No, Sir, thank you." Drazzle said.

"I could've handled them, you know." Zeet commented.

The blue jay smiled. "Maybe. But us 'specks' should watch out for one another."

The cardinal returned the smile.

Blex said to Drazzle, "Your father's looking for you, Drazzle. You'll find him at the usual place."

Drazzle nodded. "Thank you, Mr. Blex, for telling me."

Zeet, sensing his best friend's less-than-thrilled reaction to Blex's message, intervened.

"Let's go, Drazzle. I'll join you on your way."

And so, the two friends did exactly that.

Chapter 2

"Thank you for coming to the rescue, Zeet."

Zeet flew in circles around the paddling duck. "What are best friends for, anyway?" Zeet paused for a moment and said, "Say, I couldn't help but notice, this isn't the direction to go and see your dad."

Drazzle lowered his head. "I'm not quite ready to face him, Zeet."

Zeet frowned. "I thought as much."

Drazzle said, "Incidentally, I feel badly that I haven't been so talkative of late."

"When you're ready, you'll tell me what's been going on, right?"

"Yes."

"But, not yet."

Drazzle sighed. Not one caused out of irritation, just one of helplessness. How could he explain the awesome and evolving feeling within him, when he barely understood it himself?

Zeet took his cue from Drazzle's quiet introspection. "No problem, I totally understand. You know how to find me when the time's right. Take care, my friend."

And, after those spoken words, Zeet was gone. Drazzle felt even worse, because he noticed an iota undertone of hurt in Zeet's voice. In shame, the duck swam alone in a meaningless way.

Chapter 3

Indeed, while lost in his absentmindedness, Drazzle soon realized he had arrived at a section of the river devoted to the Colony's nursery.

Drazzle's mother, Vose, was in charge of the nursery of wee ducklings. The current of the river, which Drazzle did not oppose, carried him along, and he idly drifted past their play area. Drazzle watched the little ones splash and zigzag across the water. They were yellow and brown and undeniably adorable. Drazzle noticed how his mother beamed with delight as she watched over them. Her demeanor matched the jaunty pink lily flower fixed on her head. Vose's fellow caretakers matched her deportment. They appeared to be content with their lives, so why wasn't he?

When Vose took notice of him, she beckoned him to come over, with the waving of her wing.

"Hello, Drazzle," she said, in a singsong tone. "What are you doing in this area of the river? Did you know your father was looking for you?"

Drazzle nodded. "I'm aware, Mom. Mr. Blex told me."

"It's not very polite to keep him waiting, dear."

"I've...so much on my mind, Mom."

His mother looked upon him thoughtfully. "Well, I can't act surprised. Lately, you've been in your own head a lot, and mostly keeping your distance. Is there anything you'd like to talk about, Drazzle?"

Drazzle sported a reassuring smile. He even added an inflection of confidence. "No, I'm all right, Mom. But what did Dad want me for, anyway?"

Drazzle's mother squinted. She didn't fall for the pretense. Vose knew her son too well.

"*Ah,* then, it's a change of subject, is it?"

Again, Drazzle shook his head. "No, Mom. Remember, you were the one that mentioned Dad, wanting to see me."

At this, Vose chuckled. "*Touché.* Your Father is at the Mossy Boulder. He said he wants to discuss you joining the Division of Defense. After all, you are of age. Surely, you aren't surprised."

A baby duck approached them. "Nanny Vose, will you sing for me, pretty please??"

Vose regarded the duckling endearingly. "I'd be glad to, Nixie. Just please let me finish my chat with my son, here."

Drazzle took this distraction as a chance to extricate himself from the uncomfortable conversation. "Don't worry, Mom, you're working. And you already reminded me to go and see Dad. I'd best get to it. After all, as you mentioned, it's impolite to keep him waiting. See you later!"

Drazzle lovingly kissed her on the cheek, and started to swim away before she could react. Without looking back, he could his hear parent singing a song about the Grand Pilgrimage, a momentous chapter in the history of the Colony. Despite his Mother's beautiful voice, the tune made him guilty, knowing full well what the Founders had gone through to usher in happiness and safety for all the ducks.

Chapter 4

Drazzle's Father, Mez, was waiting for him at the Mossy Boulder, which was massive and submerged in the adjacent sandy bank of the river. It was the meeting place of the Division of Defense. Other members of the group were there, including some blue jays, those of whom were perched on protruding branches embedded in the soil.

Mez had just finished conversing with another duck, when he encouraged his son to approach him.

"At last, there you are, Drazzle. Where have you been, Son?"

"Just been hanging out, Dad. I haven't been doing much of anything...except for thinking."

Mez was Vose's opposite. While she was warmer, milder, Mez was stern and serious. After all, he was in charge of the Division, a position he took very earnestly.

"I've noticed," Mez began. "Which is why I think it is time for you to take your place in the Division and follow my webbed footsteps. I will instruct you in your duties. Under my guidance, you will quickly become an asset, I am certain."

"That's...great, Dad. But, to be perfectly honest, I'm not sure this is something I really want to do with my life."

Mez scrutinized him. "Expound on that, Son. Explain, then, what you want to do with your life."

"I...I don't know, Dad. I really don't."

The scrutiny continued. "Exactly. You don't know. Drazzle, you're so young. You're going through changes, and it's difficult for you to determine what you may want. You've been so distracted recently. That, and withdrawn. Quite frankly, your mother and I are worried."

No matter how strict his Father was, Drazzle knew how much he cared for him, and those last words he spoke conveyed that truth. They resonated with Drazzle. The guilt within him increased. If only Drazzle could actually articulate the strange tug he was feeling inside. He could barely make sense of it himself. One thing was sure, though, the intrinsic pull was gaining strength daily.

Lost in his labyrinth of vociferous thoughts, Drazzle inadvertently winced when Mez laid a wing on him, a gesture of fatherly support. "Son, the Division will provide you with structure, a purpose. You won't feel this adolescent confusion any more. Accept what I'm offering, and...stay."

That last word, the emphasis Mez gave it, Drazzle knew he was beginning to suspect.

"C-can I think about it, Dad? *Please*?"

Curiously, Mez relented. However, only a little.

"Of course," Mez said. "But don't dawdle too long, son. Change has a way of finding you, and you'll never know what direction it may take you."

Chapter 5

After his candid discussion with his father, Drazzle felt even more conflicted. He was alone, once more, drifting down the river. Desperately, he looked for a distraction, anything to take the growing feeling inside away. Ahead of him, he saw sunlight, dancing dazzlingly on the water. The twinkling diamond-pattern on the liquid's surface memorized him for a moment. Indeed, he was so distraction, he didn't even know he had a visitor. The voice, which startled him, brought him back to reality.

"Hello, young Drazzle."

Drazzle turned toward the sound of the voice. "Chief Founder Q'teel!"

Yes, it was, in fact, Chief Founder Q'teel. He was on the river's bank, standing between openings of thick water lilies, which showcased his presence. Spritely, he waddled to the edge of the water. Drazzle beheld his elder. His plumage was a dull white, an antique hue, and they weren't as profuse as Drazzle's. Even the orange of his bill seemed less vibrant. Notwithstanding these observations, Q'teel was seemingly not deterred by old age. His countenance was energetic.

"You've traveled far this day. You're practically in the territory of the beavers, where they've dammed up this part of the river for their lodges. Although, I reckon you've an urge to go much farther than this."

Suddenly remembering his manners, Drazzle said, "I-I'm sorry, Sir, for yelling. You surprised me, that's all. W-what can I do for you?"

"Dear boy," Q'teel began, "I'm here to help you."

"H-help me?"

11

"You bet. I've been watching you from afar. I know what's going on with you. I daresay, even your parents know. They just haven't found a way to say it yet."

Drazzle was honored, and alarmed, simultaneously. Why would the Chief Founder be interested him?? Drazzle was mediocre, unremarkable, compared to others. Surely, a most important duck such as Q'teel could find something better to do with his time.

"Your thoughts, they're so loud, I can almost hear them. Want to talk about it, Drazzle?"

Drazzle was feeling flushed. His voice trembled when he said, "I-I'm really sorry, Sir, but I must get going. My Dad wants me to join the Division of Defense, and he's expecting an answer soon. I-I'd best go and tell him what I've decided. H-have a great rest of your day, Sir!"

Drazzle flapped his wings and left the water. He looked down and saw the Chief Founder watching as he departed. Q'teel was smiling, nodding. Drazzle wondered why? Drazzle felt awful, lying to an elder, but the pressure was too great. His Mother, his Father, and now, the Chief Founder, they all wanted his attention. And, of course, something deep inside him wanted the same. Why was this happening to him??

Chapter 6

Later that night, if Drazzle had his druthers, he would have skipped out on dinner. But he felt that would have made matters even worse. Things were already awkward enough.

This side of the riverbank belonged to the Veatherbills. The three of them sat around an entrenched sizable, yet short and flat rock that resided in the middle. Atop the rock was dinner, which was comprised of small fish and worms Vose had caught, garnished with plucked grass. No one ate until Mez said the prayer of gratitude. "We give thanks to our generous river, a result of the Celestial Current, for the food we're about to gulp. Amen."

"Amen," Was said in unison, by Mez's wife and son. And soon, the food was indeed gulped.

"Delicious," said Mez.

'Yeah, it sure was." Agreed Drazzle.

"Thank you, all." Vose warmly responded.

Then, there was silence. The attention soon fell on Drazzle.

"I understand you had another run-in with those rambunctious young ducks." Mez said.

Drazzle saw a worried expression written on his mother's face. Even more so than before, actually.

Of course, Blex must have reported what he saw to Mez, Drazzle thought to himself.

"It was nothing," Drazzle said, trying to assuage his parents. "Druful and his friends were simply being their brusque selves. They only wanted to fight, because of something Zeet had said to them."

"Well, thank goodness Blex was there to stop it from becoming anything worse." Vose said.

"I agree." Said Mez.

The silence resumed itself. Until...

"So," Mez said. "What is your answer, Drazzle? Are you joining the Division?"

Drazzle was about to say something, but a visitor had made himself known.

"*Ahem!*"

The Fairfeathers looked to the direction of the sound.

"I'm sorry to come by unexpectedly, my friends, but I need to talk to you all."

Immediately, Mez and Vose waddled to the Chief Founder. With great deference, they welcomed him.

"It's a true honor, Chief Founder, to have you on our family's ground," Came from Mez.

Vose said, "Had I known you were coming, I would have prepared more food. I apologize we've no more to offer, Chief Founder."

Politely, Q'teel waved away the apology. "I'm glad I didn't interrupt your supper. I'm not here for food, anyway. Or, if I am, it's for food for thought." Amused by his own rhetoric, Q'teel lightheartedly winked at Drazzle, who was shaking inside.

"Besides, I think we all know why I'm really here." Q'teel further said, as he looked at Mez.

Mez, while trying to maintain an air of respect, announced, "Yes, I think we do. But nothing's been confirmed, and he's not leaving. He has a future with the Division."

Q'teel turned to Drazzle. "Is that so, my boy?"

Drazzle was for a loss of words. He wanted to disappear. Even more so than before.

"This is nothing to be afraid of, my friends. In fact, as you well know, it's a major part of our people's history. I'm actually surprised it hasn't appeared sooner. I reckon that's why folks around here didn't immediately see the Wanderlust in Drazzle. Complacency blinded them, I suppose. And, if so, that's why it has returned, to remind us how far we've come. We all need a good kick in our tail feathers."

"In my opinion, complacency isn't an unfortunate status. Indeed, that was the whole point of the Grand Pilgrimage, it was foundational. Moreover, I'd rather not see my son become an object lesson. There's no need for..."

Q'teel interrupted Mez. "The Wanderlust has chosen your son, Mez. It's as clear as daylight to me."

Q'teel approached Drazzle and sat next to him. "Wanderlust is like a whirlwind, the kind that scoops up the discarded leaves on the forest floor, and dances with them, scattering them about, here and there, in a lively twirl. In this example, folks, Drazzle is one of those leaves. Except this type of gust didn't touch him physically, it is all felt within. In short, the Wanderlust stirs things up, and it urges you to blow yourself in another direction, to places unknown. I should know, I felt this awe-inspiring feeling long ago."

Vose began to cry. "W-with respect, Chief Founder, your version of the Wanderlust was direly urgent. If Drazzle has it, that need doesn't exist. There's no reason for him to act on it."

"Exactly right and well said, Vose," said Mez. "My son's place is with us, amongst the Colony. You encouraged the others to follow your Wanderlust, because you were in grave peril. He's perfectly safe here, away from the Farmers and the other dangers outside our forest. And, once he's a member of the Division, he'll be instrumental in maintaining the protection for us all."

Q'teel turned to Drazzle. "Tell us, Drazzle, what does your Wanderlust feel like?"

Tears welled up in Drazzle's eyes. "I-I should've said something sooner, I know. I-I mean, I know the lessons of the Wanderlust, how could I not? It's the basis of our people. B-but what I don't understand is, why would the Wanderlust pick me out? I-I'm nothing special, I'm just an ordinary duck. That's the real reason why I kept it to myself. W-what if this is all a major mistake?"

Mez came closer. He became even more serious. "First and foremost, never talk negatively of yourself again. I won't brook it. You are our son, and you are extremely important to us."

Vose, still crying, embraced her child. "You mustn't ever think you aren't worthy of the Wanderlust. It couldn't possibly be a mistake. You're bright and capable. Wanderlust or otherwise, we love you dearly, Drazzle. Nothing will ever change that."

Drazzle burst into his tears. His Father hugged him, too. Q'teel observed silently. Consequently, he was moved by this warm sight, for his eyes glistened with tears.

Finally, he spoke, "I get what you're saying, Drazzle, I really do. I mean, back when the Wanderlust chose me, I was a young country duck, living on a farm. I was equally confused, and felt undeserving. I fought the urge to leave, I thought it was plum crazy. But...I knew staying on that farm was too dangerous. What I'm trying to say is, Drazzle, the Wanderlust gave me the courage to make a major change for myself and our kind. It wasn't easy, the pilgrimage, I'll admit it. In the end, though, the Wanderlust saved us. Maybe, my boy, you're meant to save yourself, too. Maybe you're meant to save others. You'll never know, until you accept the Wanderlust, with open wings."

Wordlessly, Drazzle took it all in, as did his parents. Q'teel words of sincerity rained over them, like a proverbial cloudburst, and it was a rich baptism of eloquence. Metaphorically speaking, they were saturated with newfound comprehension.

Mez ended the silence. "Son, is this what you really want?"

Drazzle replied, "Y-yes, Dad. I-I'm scared, but I know I-I can't ignore the Wanderlust anymore. I-I love you and Mom, and I love our home, our way of life, but...I can't stay here anymore. I-it's time to...go."

Conceding, Mez nodded. "What a brave, young duck you've become. I am so proud of you. I am sorry we didn't address this sooner." Mez looked at his wife. "We were both afraid. We were being selfish because...we didn't want to lose you."

Vose spoke. "We still don't, to be perfectly honest. But it would be wrong to hold you back. So, as hard as it is to say, you've our blessing, Drazzle."

Q'teel asked, "Would it be all right with you three if I arranged a farewell celebration? As I mentioned, the Wanderlust hasn't come for one of us in a very long time."

Mez said, "Respectfully, Chief Founder, I realize the Wanderlust beckons, yet may we have a few days to process this all? Would that also be fine with you, Drazzle?"

"Yeah, of course, Dad."

Q'teel clapped his wings. "Of course, Mez. An occasion for such a shindig shouldn't be rushed, anyhow. It deserves a right and proper recognition."

The elder read the room. At this moment, his level of enthusiasm just wasn't prevalent, nor shared.

"I reckon I'd best be off," said Q'teel. "You've got plenty to discuss. And, Drazzle, we'll have our own private conversation, well before you go. Now, I'll admit it, it's been a long time since I was outside the forest, and things have more than likely changed, but I think I can share some important life skill details."

Drazzle looked emotionally spent. Obviously, this was a lot to contend with, indeed. Reassuringly, Q'teel patted Drazzle on his shoulder.

"Just remember, Drazzle, despite the uncertainty, this is a grand new chapter and opportunity in your life, Drazzle. You should rejoice and not feel regretful.

And, with those parting words, Q'teel toddled away.

Chapter 7

No one that night had the urge or the energy to discuss the purpose of Q'teel's visit, especially since the elder had granted them time to accept and adapt to the circumstances. Everyone decided to retire for the evening, but none of them expected to fall asleep readily.

The next day, Drazzle felt he owed his best friend an explanation, so he asked Zeet to meet with him.

"So," began Zeet. "You've caught the famous Wanderlust! I've lived among the ducks long enough to know how significant such a thing like that is! Tell me all about it, Drazzle!"

Zeet's ardency was a perfect match for his plumage, bright and unapologetic. Evidently, what Drazzle had just shared with his best friend erased the patience previously extended, when Drazzle had sequestered himself from conversing with him.

Due to insomnia, Drazzle felt punchy. After Q'teel's prolific visit, he hadn't rested well. And, when sleep would finally ensnare him, it was fleeting, because the Wanderlust colored his dreams, enticing him, inspiring him, with imagery of faraway lands and watercourses. It appeared Zeet's verve was almost too much for him.

It was a beautiful and warm morning, and the two birds were in their favorite spot of the river, near a bunch of sandbar willows. They would meet here all the time to chat and hangout.

"I mean, I had no idea, you going through something so...profound. I just assumed you were going through teenage brooding. I never would've guessed it was something as awesome as Wanderlust." Zeet stroked his chin, retrospectively. "Looking back, I should've noticed, though. Come to think of it, so should have your fellow ducks."

"Well, in fairness, the Wanderlust hasn't appeared in quite a long time. But, all along, deep down, my parents knew. And, of course, I knew. It was Q'teel who had finally brought the subject to light. You know, Zeet, it was kind of liberating, getting it all out in the open. Keeping the Wanderlust inside, it was really weighing heavily on my mind, my heart."

Wide-eyed, Zeet asked, "What does Wanderlust *feel* like?"

"It's got a larger-than-life sensation," said Drazzle. "It makes you feel kind of restless. And you daydream a lot about going to other places. You have this sense that there's something else going on out there, something exciting, beyond our home. Your imagination goes into overflight."

"What do these other places look like?"

"*Oh*, other forests. Other rivers. Meeting other birds. Trying different food. Maybe meeting someone important."

Zeet looked fascinated. "You mean, a girlfriend?"

"Maybe." Drazzle's cheeks turned pink.

"I don't get it," said Zeet. "There are plenty of girl ducks here. Pretty ones, too. On my way here, I saw a *raft* of them giggling and gossiping, near a cluster of broadleaf arrowheads."

"Yeah, but none of them pay any attention to me."

The cardinal began to pace. "You sure it's Wanderlust? Maybe you're feeling something else?"

Drazzle shook his head. "Now, don't go there, Zeet. Yeah, my inadequacy is nothing new. What I'm feeling, though, it's bigger than that. And, please, don't make this any harder than it is. I know this place is great, and the

Founders worked hard to make a safe utopia for the Colony. Still, I want something..."

Zeet knowingly interjected. "More."

"Something more, yes."

"And the Chief Founder is throwing a going away party for you, Drazzle?"

Drazzle nervously laughed. "It's a little embarrassing, but, yeah, he is."

Zeet flew up and stared Drazzle directly in his eyes.

"Those girls I told you about earlier...? Well, after a big event such as that, they're gonna pay attention to you soon enough!"

Drazzle laughed and friskily swatted his best friend away, to which the cardinal evaded the playful blow.

"That won't matter, silly. Remember, I'm giving myself to the Wanderlust."

Drazzle looked to the treetops. Zeet had this notion he was seeing past them, picturing a vast, summoning sky above their forest home. "You want to know something, Zeet?"

"Sure!"

"When I said it was liberating to share the Wanderlust, realistically speaking, that was only half of it. Now, actually *leaving* my parents, you, the Colony...that's going to be the hardest part of all."

"And, letting you go," Zeet said. "It won't be easy on any of us, either."

Chapter 8

Finally, it was the morning of the big farewell party. Almost every duck was present, save for the Division of Defense members who were on duty. The event took place on the east side of the river's shore, a large and sandy section, where a thick wall of pickerelweeds grew. They had tall green stems and leaves, with purple flowers.

Q'teel was in his element. Being a master of ceremony agreed with the Chief Founder. He, Drazzle, Mez, and Vose faced their fellow ducks, all of whom were arranged in rows. In close proximity, in their own row, the other Founders were assembled.

Another point of interest was a substantial pile of nuts, berries, fish, and frogs, which were prepared in Drazzle's honor. He would have first pick at the banquet, and then, everyone else was welcome to partake.

Unmistakably, the air was abuzz with exhilaration and curiosity. Aside from them, was Druful, sulking, and didn't want to be in attendance.

Finally, Q'teel flapped his wings, and the audience hushed. All eyes were directed at him.

"Dear friends," Q'teel projected, affectionately. "A morning is symbolic of a new start. A morning is a chance to begin anew, as we shape the day, as we see fit. And, on this morning, we've gathered to celebrate a force, a feeling, which motivates new commencements."

Q'teel paused for a moment. It created an effect for the onlookers that wasn't lost on them, and the anticipation to hear more was palpable. With a voice that evoked admiration, Q'teel announced: "The Wanderlust has returned!"

A wave of reverence swept over the Colony, and immediately, the quacking of many became undiscernible, a din of passionate and growing proportion. Druful was in a state of shock. He could hardly believe what his ears had heard. He was drowning in the unwanted ardency around him.

Q'teel, using his wings, gestured in a parting manner, as if dividing water, and the crowd eventually resumed their composure. Again, the Chief Founder had the floor.

"As it chose me, all those years ago, this time, it has come for our very own, Drazzle Fairfeather."

The elder acknowledged Drazzle, with a slow nod, and Drazzle reciprocated.

"We've no idea where the Wanderlust will take him, but I reckon the purpose will become very clear, once it steers his actions and he arrives at his destination point. Drazzle's parents, Mez and Vose, they've bestowed their blessing to their only child. It wasn't an easy decision for them, yet they know and recognize the power of the Wanderlust. They understand and accept Drazzle's destiny lies elsewhere. A round of applause, please, for the bravery of their approval!"

Everyone clapped, even Druful's friends, much to his dismay. Mez and Vose were gladdened by the ovation. Holding wings, they bowed. Mez looked really proud, while Vose, she shed tender tears.

"Drazzle, my boy, I know you're overwhelmed. How could you not be? Saying goodbye, and going on a trip, they're not easy things to consent to. Nevertheless, you must trust the Wanderlust. Without it, I wouldn't be standing here today. The Colony would not have ever existed. Look at what flowered, after a difficult and uncertain decision to leave that farm, to putting the

Farmers far behind us. We've a wonderful home, we're safe and sound."

Q'teel took a moment and surveyed his onlookers. It was an expression an artist would display, after completing something truly meaningful. The elder continued his speech.

"I reckon, it makes one wonder, doesn't it? Why would the Wanderlust come again, after all these years? In my view, I think it's a cue to our past, and a reason to appreciate what we've got, here and now. That's only part of it, though. The Wanderlust has something important for you to do, Drazzle, and there's no such thing as coincidence. It's gusting inside you for a purpose. Let it guide you, my boy. You've got a great mind and a caring heart, you'll prosper, and I just know it!"

More clapping resounded. "I've talked enough, I think. Mez? Vose? I'm sure you've things to say to your son."

Mez said, "You have always made me proud, Drazzle. Today, despite the pain of letting you go, you have taken that to an apex level. I wish you very well, son. Remember what I told you, Drazzle, you are worthy of the Wanderlust. Serve it well, and it shall do the same for you. I love you."

Mez embraced his son. After he released Drazzle, his mother approached. She held her wingtips in a prayer position as she sobbed.

"M-my baby," she said, with a quaking voice. "I'm going to miss you tremendously. Y-you mean the world to us. Carry our love with you, Drazzle, and I hope and pray we will see you again, and you'll regale us with your adventure. B-but...if not...I wish for you a happy, fulfilled life."

She hugged him, as if there was no tomorrow. They both were crying. Affectionately, Mez placed a wing over his wife. In response, she set free Drazzle, and took comfort in her husband's cuddle.

"And now," began Q'teel, "Let's hear from the Duck of Honor."

Q'teel and his parents took a step back. Drazzle had the spotlight. It was a little unnerving, facing so many, and he had never engaged in public speaking before. But these were his people, there was no reason to be afraid. Finally, he found his voice.

"For the life of me, I've no idea why I was selected by the Wanderlust. It's a mystery to me. In fact, an agonizingly confusing one. I should have spoken up far sooner when I first felt it, but fear held me back. Not only fear, but guilt. Our Founders endured a lot to establish our way of life. What was wrong with *me*, to want to leave here? It's ironic: Chief Founder Q'teel took the others away from the farm for the sake of a better existence. That was the nature of his Wanderlust. As for mine, in the Colony, I already have a safe and caring existence, yet I'm feeling a powerful need to leave. I...I want something more. I apologize if that seems selfish to you, I really do. And, as intimidating as the prospect is, it's time for me to see this through, all alone."

Unexpectedly, Zeet flew down into view. In midflight, he addressed Drazzle.

"There's no need to be alone, Drazzle. If you'll have me, I'm willing to come along, too!"

"Zeet, that's very...are you sure?? You'd be leaving behind your own family, your own home!"

"Here's the interesting thing about this Wanderlust, Drazzle. Evidently, it's contagious. Since you talked about it, I've caught the feeling, as well! And, like you, I'm old enough to make my own decisions. I'm in!"

Puzzled, Drazzle looked at Q'teel. "Chief Founder, is such a thing possible? Can you *catch* Wanderlust?"

Q'teel smiled and gestured toward the other Founders. "You tell me." The elder replied.

Drazzle felt an intrinsic pang of embarrassment, quickly recalling his audience, all of whom, incidentally, except for Druful, were watching with astonishment.

"O-of course, Sir. I completely understand." Said Drazzle.

Mez came forward. "What about Zeet, son? May he join you on your journey?"

Silence fell on everyone present, so much so, you could have heard a pinecone drop. Drazzle locked eyes with his father. Mez did not flinch. Drazzle shifted his focus to his mother, whom, parenthetically, was awaiting Drazzle's reply with abated breath.

"Absolutely!"

Zeet was elated. The spectators cheered. "Well, then," said Q'teel. "Let's start this party! Drazzle —and Zeet—it's your special day, you may eat first! Next, his parents, followed by the Founders, and after that, everyone else! Enjoy!"

Zeet landed on Drazzle's back as the duck waddled towards the food. Midway, though, Zeet got his attention.

"Say, Drazzle, do you remember what I said about getting the girls' attention?"

"Yeah, sure, what of them?"

"Look behind you."

Drazzle paused and glanced behind him. Indeed, he noticed them gazing, all starry-eyed. Drazzle blushed and continued moving.

Druful addressed his buddies. "C'mon, guys, let's get out of here. *Guys*?"

Druful saw his friends getting in line for the banquet. It angered him. Swiftly, he tried to retake his influence over them. "Hey, guess what! I think *I'm* feeling the Wanderlust, too!"

Druful's friends turned around, briefly, and pivoted back towards the direction of the food.

Druful knew when he was licked. He joined his friends.

Chapter 9

As the banquet started to wind down, Q'teel reassumed a point of emphasis. "Dear friends, as I walked among you, it was really wonderful to hear such spirited conversations. Some were nostalgic, while others looked to the future. And speaking of the future, it's time for these two vessels of the Wanderlust to embrace theirs. Drazzle and Zeet, come forward and stand before me."

The two young birds obeyed. Q'teel spread his old wings wide. He thrust his head, and closed his eyes and entreated aloud, "Wanderlust, whisk away your chosen and deliver them safely to new destinies."

Q'teel reopened his eyes, which were energized with potential and exhilaration. "It's time for you to ascend. The Colony wishes you well, and we all know you'll make us proud. Remember what we discussed in private—and beware of the Farmers, always. Now, go. Your new lives await!"

Drazzle and Zeet bowed. Next, they looked at one another, nodded, and slowly, yet surely, took flight. As they rose, they looked down at everyone. Avidly, they applauded and cheered. Drazzle saw his parents, embraced, watching proudly. And soon, Drazzle and Zeet crossed the aperture among the profuse foliage. Below them, it looked like an extensive and verdant ceiling. They found themselves surrounded by a vast blue sky, flecked with gray-white clouds of myriad shapes and sizes.

"So," wondered Zeet. "Where does the Wanderlust want us to go from here?"

Drazzle looked to his right, and then, to the left. Finally, he said, "Let's fly in that direction—south—I'm feeling a core yank in that direction!"

And so, they did.

Chapter 10

It was two days ago since their fond farewell party from their dense forest home, and while the Wanderlust provided encouragement, Drazzle and Zeet still required food and rest. They chose to land on a grassy meadow, one which had a stream flowing through it. Drazzle skidded on the water, and created a splash. Hungry, he quested after tadpoles, snails, and underwater vegetation. Alternatively, Zeet took his nourishment from a bountiful blueberry bush.

After the friends finished lunch, and Drazzle was still floating in the water, while Zeet was perched on a small tree branch, which was nearby the stream, it was a practical stance for the both of them. Zeet took the high ground, looking out for trouble. In turn, Drazzle observed the low ground, doing the same. Before Drazzle left, Q'teel cautioned Drazzle to savor his new surroundings, but to always stay vigilant and diligent. Now, far away from the watchful eye of the Division of Defense, they were vulnerable to danger. Drazzle called to the cardinal.

"Do you see anything?"

Effortlessly, Zeet leaped branch to branch. "From up here, everything looks clear. What about you?"

"It's equally clear down here. It appears we have the meadow entirely to ourselves. There's no sign of foxes or Farmers."

"Thank goodness!" chirped Zeet.

"Still," Drazzle said. "We mustn't lower our guard. Foxes are sly, sneaky things. Tragically, on the Grand Pilgrimage, all those years ago, Q'teel told me some of the ducks were snatched by those red-orange monsters."

Zeet shuddered. "They're the stuff of nightmares. What did Q'teel say of the Farmers?"

"Believe it or not, they're even scarier, and more powerful. Q'teel said they can harness the power of thunder itself!"

Zeet sputtered a rebuttal. "You're pulling my twiggy leg!"

Somberly, Drazzle shook his head. "Once, on the Grand Pilgrimage, Q'teel and the others stopped for a rest. They found a spacious lake. Unfortunately, secretly lurking, some Farmers lured a few of the ducks away, using our *own* language!"

Zeet crotched. "Y-you're saying they spoke Duckish?"

"Yes, and once they knew they had been tricked, by a false bidding, those ducks tried to get away—but they were felled by the thunder in the Farmers' hands! Q'teel said it was a terrible sound, much like the end of the world!"

A shiver entered Zeet's body. "How awful. I thought thunder was the result of the sky breaking."

Drazzle was impressed. Although a cardinal, Zeet took and accepted the beliefs of the Colony for himself.

"You're right. Hidden behind in the sky lies an infinite Celestial Current. It is responsible for all the water in the corporeal world. When a duck dies, its soul goes and joins the Celestial Current, forever swimming in tranquility. Yes, the Current's hiding place is boundless, but it's also delicate. Occasionally, openings form and the water will fall to the realm below. Sometimes, the ruptures are violent, hence the thunder and the lightning. Overall, whether it be a mizzle or a thundershower, the rainfall is a boon. It renews the millponds, the lakes, all the water sources."

Zeet hung on every word, as if he were hearing this sermon for the very first time. "*Gosh*, I wondered how the

Farmers mastered such a remarkable feat, making the thunder theirs!"

"Who can say for sure? It's a disturbing mystery for us. Farmers are such crafty creatures. I sincerely hope the Wanderlust steers us safely away from them."

Zeet hopped in a zigzag and mimicked the movement of a streaking lightning bolt. "I hope they haven't learned how to use noisy thunder's electrical companion, too!"

Drazzle winced, as he imagined such a distressing supposition. "Yes, I agree."

Suddenly, the serenity of the meadow seemed rather scary. All this talk about the Farmers had decidedly spooked them both. At the Colony, when the leaves of the trees would assume the fiery colors of a summer sunset, the ducks of Drazzle's age would tell each other scary stories about the infamous Farmers.

Across the stream, against the sunlight, the weeping willow tree took on an eerie silhouette effect, which made it look enormously wraithlike. Except for the occasional sound of a stiff breeze, an abundance of deafening silence prevailed. Since their exit from home, the euphoria of the Wanderlust kept them enthralled and enthused. However, in the middle of nowhere, it truly dawned on the feathered pair that they were alone, away from everyone and everything they ever knew.

"I don't think we should delay the Wanderlust any longer, Zeet. If you're ready, let's go."

"No argument from me, Drazzle."

Immediately, they took to the sky, and they didn't look back.

Chapter 11

An hour after the two friends had left the meadow, while still in transit in the air, Drazzle looked at his traveling companion. He watched how his wings flapped, like red blurs. Notwithstanding his diminutive size, the cardinal kept up with Drazzle's flight speed rather energetically. Indeed, there was no shortage to Zeet's dynamism. And, consequently, having admitted that to himself, Drazzle wondered how easily it would be to motivate such a personality into doing something new and bold.

"Zeet, do you mind if I ask you a question? Something, admittedly, I should've asked you sooner?"

"Not at all, go right ahead, Drazzle."

"Did my father ask you to come with me? Or, was it possibly my mother? Maybe, even, was it Q'teel himself?"

Zeet was abnormally speechless. He took on a contemplative expression, as if he was trying to work out the best thing to say. Finally, he said, "OK, I don't actually have a case of the Wanderlust, like you do, but you understood what Q'teel said about the elders. They *caught* his inspiration. It was the same thing for me, I guess."

It was Drazzle's turn to ponder. What Zeet revealed, it made sense, and it was convincing. But Drazzle knew his best friend all too well. There was something more, he simply sensed it, despite Zeet's best attempt at an explanation.

"After your announcement about the Wanderlust being contagious, I saw something in my father's eyes. It was insistence. It was all about you joining me on my trip. I'm sorry, I really should've brought this up sooner, but it's something I must know. So, then, am I right? Did my father ask you to come along?"

Zeet's orange beak yawned open, an effect of surprise. "I-I don't understand why you're even wondering about this! I'm here, aren't I? Does it matter if he did or didn't ask me? We're together, that's what should count!"

Zeet was on the borderline of being flabbergasted. Rarely, they ever truly quarreled, and Drazzle wouldn't hurt Zeet's feelings for the world, yet he had to know the truth.

"Zeet, please, in respect to our friendship, just be honest with me."

Zeet registered the serious tone in the duck's voice. He buckled and said, "All right, fine, yeah, your father asked me to fly away with you."

Drazzle wasn't exactly all that astounded by the confession. "I see."

"As the Director of the Division of Defense, Mez has a lot of clout."

"But you aren't even a member of the Division."

"Still, that clout counts. Knowing I'm your best friend, Mez didn't want you to go it alone. I imagine your mother felt exactly the same, and I wouldn't be shocked at all if she didn't have a say in this matter."

Zeet stopped talking for a moment. He flew closer to Drazzle. "Are you mad at me?"

"Not at all. The reason why I pressed you so hard for an answer was, why did my father think I wasn't capable of doing this by myself?"

"Drazzle, if he thought you couldn't, he would've grounded this journey from the get-go. All he wanted for you was to have a little company, figuratively and literally."

Zeet's joke made Drazzle laugh. "I suppose you're right."

"Sure, I am! I mean, Mez could've asked a blue jay from the Division to tag along—he had plenty of choices—but that would've been too impersonal. Instead, he chose someone friendly and familiar. So, yes, there was another element to my own Wanderlust. Yet, to be perfectly honest, I would've missed you a lot, so I'm glad I accepted Mez's request. When you first got the Wanderlust, we weren't spending all that much time together, anyhow. This way, we can make up for lost time, and we are!"

Drazzle smiled. "I'm truly glad you accepted, too, Zeet."

Spiritedly, Zeet flitted. "My performance was so masterfully convincing, even Q'teel wasn't aware of your father's role in my choice."

Drazzle thought differently. Similar to his parents, maybe the Chief Founder suspected Mez's handiwork and chose not to expose it. After all, when the elder had the Wanderlust, he left the farm in the company of dozens of ducks. He did not seek a new life unaccompanied. As such, Q'teel understood the need for comradeship. And, having Zeet around, it gladdened Drazzle's heart tenfold.

Chapter 12

The next day, after days of flying, the pair of vagabonds decided to take a rest in a sizable hardwood swamp. Bulging from the water, there were elms, silver maple, and red maple trees. Patches of wide and thick pond scum, bright green in color, blanketed sections of the swamp's surface. A surfeit of emerald-green lily pads could be seen from any direction.

Zeet, amongst this viridescent environment, was almost glowing, a ruby-feathered focal point. He was perched on a cattail, which, given his position and the breaths of the wind, caused it to bob.

Drazzle, with sheer delight, was savoring the plentiful feast of pondweed. He would plunge his neck beneath the blue-black water, leaving his tail feathers monetarily perpendicular, with his orange legs pedaling. He repeated this action several times. Zeet was steadfast in his vigilance while Drazzle ate.

Once his appetite was satisfied, Drazzle said, "It's your turn to look for food."

Zeet smiled. "You look very happy, Drazzle."

Drazzle reflected Zeet's smile. "This place is lovely."

Zeet jumped to another cattail. "Is this it, then? Is this where the Wanderlust wants us to stay?"

Drazzle closed his eyes and engaged in some introspection. He then opened them and shook his damp head. "I don't think so, Zeet. Inside, the Wanderlust is as gusty as ever. I can feel it spinning, tugging, and longing for something that awaits me." Drazzle corrected himself. "I mean, us."

"But, as we established, the Wanderlust isn't inside me."

Graciously, Drazzle extended a wing, an act of camaraderie. "You're with me, and that's more than enough."

Zeet blushed, a shade of violet, clearly touched by his best friend's sincerity. Zeet said, "So our adventure continues."

"Yeah, you bet. For now, though, let's enjoy the nostalgia that this swamp proffers. Look around—the greenery, the dim lighting—they all remind me of home."

For a moment, Drazzle fell silent, lost in his own reminiscence. Drazzle pictured his parents. In his heart, he knew they were missing him as much as he was missing them. He envisioned the old river and how many times he sailed it. No matter how much the Wanderlust craved something new for his life, Drazzle was truly beginning to recognize the importance of his previous domicile and the family which provided it meaning.

Zeet saw the duck drifting down his own river of musing.

"Cardinal to duck, Drazzle, cardinal to duck, come back to me."

Drazzle blinked and returned to the here-and-now. "I'm sorry, Zeet. You're probably so hungry, you'd best find something to eat for yourself."

"You'll be all right? Remember, Q'teel said to always stay alert. If you get lost in a daydream…"

"I'll be fine. Go and eat."

Zeet gave him one last glance, nodded, and flew towards the red maple. Drazzle watched as his friend was seemingly absorbed by the scarlet leaves, like a disappearing act. Drazzle hoped his friend would find lots of tasty insects to eat.

Chapter 13

Meantime, it was up to Drazzle to remain conscientious regarding his surroundings. As such, he saw something small and black flying, quickly approaching. The newcomer landed on a lopsided old log. Despite his size, which wasn't much bigger than Zeet, Drazzle kept his guard up.

"Hello, there! I'm Wost, a lifelong denizen of the Flooded Forest. For generations, my kind have served as patrollers. Do you see my badge? It represents my hereditary prestige."

Drazzle noticed how Wost had angled himself horizontally, a means of displaying his left wing, which featured something resembling an emblem. The upper part of this motif was reddish-orange, while the lower section was yellow, a pleasing dichotomy, Drazzle had thought to himself.

"Your badge is wonderful. Also, I'm so glad you understand Duckish, so we may talk. Tell me, Wost, you said you're a patroller. What does that mean?" Said Drazzle.

Wost was noticeably flattered. "Thank you for the compliment. As for my role, we scout the Flooded Forest and we look for newcomers and investigate their intentions. As for your language, I've seen my share of ducks and geese before, but I must admit, though, I've never seen a duck as white as you. From afar, I thought you were a cloud and had fallen into the water and had gotten stuck in the muck."

"We're even, then. I've never met someone such as you previously. In fact, with respect, may I please ask you what you are?"

Proudly, the bird stated, "I'm a red-winged blackbird."

Drazzle smiled. "That makes sense. How nice. My name is Drazzle Fairfeather, by the way."

The blackbird returned the smile "It's a pleasure to meet you, Drazzle. The Flooded Forest is a home for many birds. Will you be staying here indefinitely? Is that your intention?"

"I'm afraid not. My friend and I are just passing through."

Wost looked about. "I see no one else."

Using his wing, Drazzle pointed to the red maple tree. "My friend, Zeet, he's a cardinal, and he's having his lunch. He should be along soon. I'll be happy to introduce you."

Wost cocked his head. Something else had caught his attention. Drazzle saw what was approaching them.

A lanky bird was strutting across the water. Its upper body was entirely white. Its neck was golden and wrinkled. Its beak was long and curved at the end, a bronze color. Using its grey, long and thin legs, the mystery bird sauntered towards Wost. Using its wings and facial expressions, a message was being nonverbally distributed, one of which Wost paid attention to intently.

"Thanks for the update, Strattonash. *Oh*, lest I forget, this is Drazzle. He's only here temporarily."

Strattonash bowed. Drazzle did the same. "He's in the company of a cardinal named Zeet. If you want to add that to your bulletin, then there you go."

Strattonash smiled, then turned, and wandered away. Drazzle looked as he paused and dipped his beak in the water, a seeking method, it appeared to Drazzle, and a most successful one, too, for he had caught a fish, easily, and swallowed it whole.

Drazzle reverted his attention to Wost, whom, incidentally, was looking pensive.

"Mr. Wost, is everything all right? It's obvious Strattonash has you worried about something, even though he said nothing."

Wost said, ""*Oh*, trust me, he said plenty. Where you're from, do have storks?"

"I'm afraid not, Sir."

"I see. Well, Drazzle, Strattonash is a mute stork. To communicate, he uses gestures and facial expressions. Storks are excellent at making deliveries, particularly with news good or bad."

Drazzle looked concerned. "I take it Strattonash had bad news to share."

The blackbird's expression turned grim. "Not too far away from here, there was a hawk sighting."

Zeet rejoined Drazzle. "Hey, who's this?"

"Zeet, this is Wost. He's one of the Flooded Forest's patrollers. Wost, meet Zeet. Wost just received some bad news."

"*Gee*, I'm sorry to hear that. What's up?" asked Zeet.

"*What's up*? That's a very good question to ask, Zeet, because it is what comes from above that we must fear." Wost looked back and forth, as he searched the immense blue overhead. Zeet and Drazzle followed his example.

Evidently, satisfied with his evaluation of the ether, Wost continued to explain.

"A hawk was spotted nearby, on the border of the swamp. It's not safe for us to be exposed like this, boys. If I were you, I'd seek some shelter. Given your whiteness, Drazzle, you'll be quite visible to it, a sitting duck, if you'll excuse the phrasing. The same goes for Zeet, given his red feathers. I'd recommend losing yourselves deeper inside the Flooded Forest. It's right over there, to your left."

Drazzle and Zeet turned and saw a plethora of sunken trees.

"As for me, I'm going back to my nest." Wost announced.

"Wait, please," Drazzle pleaded. "Before you go, what *is* a hawk??"

Wost lowered his vocal register, almost to a whisper, as if he didn't want the dreaded topic at hand to overhear his interpretation. It made the situation even more suspenseful. "A hawk is monster, a demon, a cannibal—a bird that eats other birds, among other creatures! From overhead, it launches an attack! It has keen eyesight, sharp talons, and a jagged beak, which it uses to tear open its victims!"

Drazzle recoiled. "A bird that *eats* other birds??"

Wost shrugged and said, "It's not unheard of. Even storks will make a meal out of a small bird."

The blackbird studied their faces, which were discernable with confusion. "Maybe it *is* unheard, after all. Anyway, you really should find some shelter. A hawk moves quickly, and it could be upon us at any given moment. I hope we'll meet again. Goodbye, and good luck."

Wost dashed away. Drazzle and Zeet shared apprehensive gazes, and then they looked above, afraid to see an actual nightmare soaring, searching for its next prey, and skedaddled to Wost's suggested sanctuary.

Chapter 14

Inside the Flooded Forest, Drazzle and Zeet took refuge under a buttonbush, which was richly green, and was embellished with flowers that were spherical in shape, a yellow-white hue, with protruding thin white shoots, tipped in yellow tiny tops.

Conveniently, Zeet discovered an aperture in the wall of their leafy haven. Considering the cardinal's size, it was an ideal spyhole. Since they were hiding, the two friends decided it was best to communicate by whispering.

"What I don't get," Zeet began, "is why Wost would be friends with someone that could eat him? I mean, what makes Strattonash so special, and this hawk thing such a threat?"

Drazzle gave it some careful thought. "Maybe, for some, friendship can supersede basic survival needs. Maybe they arrived at a mutual agreement. Take the Colony and the blue jays, for example. Weren't they different themselves? Yet, they managed to find common ground and form an alliance. Now, aside from necessity, I guess friendships come in many forms. Consider us, Zeet. To some, we might be an odd pairing. Back home, there were plenty of other ducks my own age, yet I couldn't relate to them. It didn't matter to me you were a cardinal, because you were the only one I really identified with."

"Ditto, all the way. My fellow cardinals, they were cool, but they weren't you. I mean, you understood me better than they could. Yes, I totally get what you're saying. Still, we never saw one another as a potential meal."

"True. I suppose, after all that time we lived in isolation in the Colony, we've a lot to learn about the outside world." Drazzle admitted.

"So, speaking of what's outside, are you scared?"

"Yeah, definitely. You and I, we've never faced such a challenge before. But I believe in the Wanderlust. It chose me for a purpose. It will deliver us to safety, I must believe this."

Zeet regarded the duck. Under this encompassing shroud of foliage, the visibility was diminished. For a moment, given the wisdom—and the faith—which both underscored his friend's words, in the dimness, which dulled Drazzle's youthful white plumage, it was as if Q'teel had traded places with Drazzle. Of course, Zeet knew better. Indeed, it was such a contrast, Zeet continued to pond how far Drazzle had come, literally and figuratively, since accepting the bestowment of the Wanderlust. Zeet recalled the confusion and conflict that preoccupied Drazzle, going insofar as to isolate himself from those who cared about him the most. That time was behind Drazzle, the denial was gone, because, even under the prospect of peril, he was a proud proponent of the boon that his people revered. He intended to see the purpose of the Wanderlust through, come what may.

Zeet took another glimpse through the peephole. "*Uh-oh.*"

"What's the matter, Zeet? Is...is it the hawk?"

"Nope," said Zeet. "It's something else. Kind of reminds me of a beaver, except this thing has a longer, thinner body."

"Let me see." Drazzle waddled over and squinted through the opening. Sure enough, Drazzle saw the stranger, swimming, seemingly blithely aware of impending danger.

"Zeet," said Drazzle, with a tone riddled with concern, "I don't think it knows about the hawk. It seems so carefree. Just look at it."

Somberly, Zeet nodded. "You're probably right."

"I'm going to warn it," Drazzle decided.

"Are you crazy?? You don't know that thing—it could be just as dangerous as the hawk!"

"We don't know that! If not for Wost and Strattonash, we would've been out there, oblivious and vulnerable! It's only fair—and right—to pass on the warning." When Drazzle spoke again, it was no longer a whisper. He yelled through the wall of greenery.

"Hey, you! Yes, you! You're in danger, you need to hide, right now!"

Drazzle watched the confounded creature, clearly startled by his shouting voice that, to it, had materialized from nowhere. Consequently, it disappeared beneath the murky water.

The next thing the two friends knew, their buttonbush shelter was being savaged from above. Ruthlessly, talons tore it to shreds. Daylight shown through the breaches. Something large was pouncing aerially and relentlessly. The din of the plant's razing, as well as the beating of mighty wings, was all quite distressing.

Zeet exclaimed, "Drazzle, you kindhearted dummy, you gave us away!"

Drazzle matched Zeet's scream, "Zeet, get out of here!!"

Zeet, being smaller, made his escape from the other side of the buttonbush. In turn, Drazzle fled for the water. Drazzle's protagonist took notice of Drazzle's exit and went skyward. From below, Drazzle got a good look at the marauder. The hawk was powerfully built, large, and colored white and butterscotch. Its tail feathers were red.

Its beak, which was menacingly curved, looked like an extra talon, and it was just as sharp.

"I was in the mood for a muskrat for supper, but you spoiled that! You'll have to take its place!"

Drazzle, not knowing the hawk's language, only heard strident screeches, but the ire in its voice was unmistakable.

With determination, with preternatural speed, the hawk descended. Instead of snatching Drazzle, it only skidded the surface of the water, with a substantial splish-splash. Drazzle knew this was a near miss, and his foe was again midair, preparing for another assault. Frantically, Drazzle recalled what the Division of Defense had taught him, and he moved, to-and-fro, frantically splashing, which prevented the hawk from getting too close. Obviously vexed by Drazzle's splattering tactic, the hawk flew nearby diagonally, tenaciously.

Drazzle knew what he was doing was transitory. Eventually, his erratic repelling would give way to fatigue. Then he would be helpless. Ergo, he opted to go underwater. Drazzle suspected his adversary's province was the sky and ground, but not water. Drazzle dove deeply, as far as he could. This, too, was a fleeting maneuver, knowing full well that his lungs would eventually demand oxygen.

Accordingly, Drazzle resurfaced haphazardly, taking a swift breath, and once more, he submerged himself. Whenever he reappeared, Drazzle saw the hawk relentlessly spiraling overhead.

Zeet, who had perched himself on the branch of an adjacent elm tree, wasn't content to idly standby and watch while the hawk hunted his best friend. Desperately, he jumped up and down, flapped his wings, as he tried earnestly to serve as a distraction.

"Leave him alone, you ugly beast!" Zeet yelled, with all his might.

Of course, the hawk noticed Zeet's display and retorted, but never deviated from his pursuit of Drazzle.

"Ordinarily, I'd have you for an appetizer. After I eat this duck, you'll be my dessert!"

Like Drazzle beforehand, Zeet had no idea what was said to him, only that it was delivered in a rude, taunting tone. Discouraged that the hawk didn't take him for another target, Zeet observed the hawk. He could tell the fiend was studying Drazzle's pop-goes-the-weasel routine, judging when best to strike. When Drazzle reemerged, the hawk was ready for him. Drazzle watched in horror, as the instrument of his death was aiming for him, with its claws pointed forward. Its expression was terrifyingly fixated.

Chapter 15

Dozzy couldn't bear to keep his eyes open. He heard Zeet's anguished protesting. In his mind, random moments of his life paraded. He saw his parents, Mez and Vose, loving and dedicated, swimming with him on a lovely spring day, when he was a duckling, and recollected how safe he felt with them; and then, there was Q'teel , sagely spinning yarns about the Grand Pilgrimage; next, he saw himself in Mr. Poom's class, on the beginning day of school, and was brought to mind how nervous he felt; and he recalled meeting Zeet for the first time, and instantly befriending him; and he remembered the day he initially felt the Wanderlust, and how it turned his life upside-down; and finally, with Zeet, he watched himself ascend from the Colony's farewell party, the morning he followed the Wanderlust to wherever he was meant to go. More images of his past manifested, but amalgamated in a colossal kaleidoscope, indistinguishable.

Oddly enough, oblivion was tardy. There was no pain from piercing talons, or a raking beak. Did the hawk miss?! But how?!! It was coming straight for him!

Drazzle's wild ruminations were halted by Zeet's cheering. He heard Zeet calling to him, urging him to open his eyes, which, ultimately, he did, and was astonished by the sight that befell him. It became clear to Drazzle why the hawk's trajectory was interrupted.

A group of birds, much larger than Wost, were dive-bombing the hawk. Unlike Wost, these newcomers were entirely black. Using teamwork, they took turns targeting Drazzle's would-be killer. These other birds were noisy, and, even though he couldn't decipher their language, which sounded like throaty *cawings*, there was something familiar about it that reminded of him of the blue jays he knew in the Division of Defense.

Chapter 16

Thankfully, these birds were only interested in the hawk, whom, incidentally, was overburdened, because when it tried to repel one pecking attacker, another one would appear and persisted. Outnumbered and seeing no alternative, and not wanting to be harassed any further, the hawk fled. Boisterously, the blackbirds pursued.

Zeet flew to Drazzle and hugged his neck. "Drazzle, thank goodness you're all right!"

In turn, Drazzle embraced the cardinal. "I'm so grateful to be here!"

Drazzle released Zeet, and the latter landed on his head. Zeet said, "Now, that we've gotten the thankfulness out of the way..." The cardinal smartly pecked the duck's dome.

"*Ow*! What was that for??" Drazzle snapped, as he rubbed his sore spot.

Zeet took flight again and hovered before his accuser. "Because you were reckless earlier! By warning that...beaver-like thing...the hawk found us, and it almost had you, too."

Drazzle retorted, "So, then, I was supposed to stay quiet and let another living thing get killed??"

"Again, that living thing could have been dangerous to us, as much as the hawk. We were already in danger. You could've made everything worse. Also, for your trouble, did you notice the furry animal never even thanked you?"

Drazzle said, stormily, "First, when I shouted my warning, I scared it—you saw that yourself—so, it was no wonder it fled, before it offered any appreciation. I wasn't looking for that, anyway. I just wanted to do the right thing. Second, the Wanderlust selected me for something special, as it did Q'teel, many years ago. I hardly think it wouldn't have bothered to gust its way into my soul, only to reduce me to be someone's lunch. As I told you, Zeet, I believe in the Wanderlust. And, I thought you did, too."

Zeet's voice lowered, "I wouldn't be here, Drazzle, if I didn't. More importantly, I believe in *you*. But you must think of the Grand Pilgrimage. Not all the ducks that left the farm with Q'teel made it to the intended destination point. The Wanderlust failed to protect them, didn't it?"

Drazzle was rendered speechless. Once more, Zeet took the knowledge of Drazzle's people and hurled it back at him. Still, along with this point Zeet had made so stingingly, Drazzle felt it was his turn to make one of his own.

"Are you more worried about yourself, I gather?" Drazzle said. "I can't believe what I'm hearing from you. Whatever happened to my spunky friend, the one who was prepared to take on Druful and his gang of bullies? Then, you supported defending a victim, such as myself, why not extend that altruism to someone else?"

Zeet shook his head. "You're not a victim, and you never were. By helping you, being there for you, those were acts of friendship. Q'teel would probably call it a good deed."

"And, in essence, Zeet, that's what I was trying to accomplish, a good deed for a stranger."

"I get it. I really do. All I'm saying, Drazzle, is to not rely on the Wanderlust entirely. As impressive and important as it is, it's not foolproof. We've got to look out for each other. We're far from home, and we must be smart about things, especially strangers."

"Well, I get what you're telling me, too." Drazzle said. "I don't regret helping the furry one. I still insist I did the right thing."

"And, I don't regret sharing you my feelings."

Drazzle detected the equivalent fervor demonstrated in Zeet's voice. None of them intended to budge. It felt like an impasse. "Shall we agree to disagree, then?"

Laconically, Zeet said, "Yeah."

Since the inception of their fellowship, this was the fieriest divergence of ideology to ever stand between them. The previous scrutiny of Zeet, regarding Drazzle's father's part in the cardinal's choice to join him on his trip, paled in comparison to this dissimilarity of duty, even though it almost fell on the borderline of discord.

Fortunately, the subject wasn't addressed any further, due to the timely arrival of two familiar visitors.

"I'm so relieved to see you're all right!" Wost said.

Drazzle and Zeet turned and saw them approaching. Wost was standing on the back of Strattonash, who was trudging through the water.

"Wost—Strattonash—we're equally glad to see you, too." Said Drazzle.

"As Strattonash will attest, news can travel as fast as wind. Other patrollers saw a *murder* of crows had entered the section of the Flooded Forest. In turn, the storks learned of this and shared the update, which Strattonash passed on to me. An 'all clear' status was declared. That's why we're here to check up on you boys. Are you all right?"

Drazzle wasn't too thrilled with the designation for the crows. It sounded ominous to him.

"Drazzle wouldn't have been, if not for the timely arrival of those—what did you call 'em?—crows. They saved Drazzle." Zeet said.

At this, Strattonash gained additional vigor. To him, this sounded like even more stimulating news. Wost was able to remain more objective.

"Boys, I'm sorry to molt your feathers, but that wasn't a rescue. You see, crows hate hawks, and the feeling is mutual, believe me. Crows are known for being territorial. That's why they appeared and got rid of the hawk. They must be moving in to the Flooded Forest."

"Will that be a problem?" Drazzle asked.

"It could be. But, for today, I'm just grateful they took care of the hawk. You are one lucky duck, Drazzle."

"With respect, Mr. Wost, it wasn't luck that saved me, it was the Wanderlust."

Strattonash was intrigue. Wost matched the stork's interest. "Never heard of it, what's that?"

"You attributed a news bulletin to the wind. Where I'm from, my people consider Wanderlust to be a fateful, spiritual gust of wind that chooses a duck and blows him in a new direction in life. That's what I meant when I said we're passing through. We're following it to wherever it leads us. And, based on how I still feel inside, the Flooded Forest isn't the right place."

Wost acknowledged, "I get what you're saying...to an extent. What I don't fully understand is, Zeet is not a duck. Drazzle, you specifically mentioned ducks. How, then, does Zeet have it?"

Strattonash was eager to hear the answer, given his attentiveness to the conversation.

"While it's true," Drazzle began, "Zeet doesn't have it in the same sense. He's uplifted by friendship and inspiration, an offshoot of the Wanderlust. It has united us in a special way. No matter what, we are on this journey together."

Drazzle intentionally regarded Zeet. It was Drazzle's way of apologizing, without actually saying it in the conventional sense. It was a means of reaffirming their concord. Zeet, getting the gist, articulated his approval with a nod.

Wost said, "Fascinating. You, and Zeet, and this Wanderlust, you're all about to become facets of the history of the Flooded Forest. After all, knowing Strattonash as well as I do, the news will spread to everyone living here. Moreover, you'll be celebrated, because it's not every day a duck waddles away from a hawk attack—not to mention a gang of crows—unscathed."

Drazzle shared, "Actually, not all of us made it out unscathed. Not everyone was as fortunate we were."

Zeet, Wost, and Strattonash followed Drazzle's line of vision, which led them to the ruined buttonbush, Drazzle and Zeet's makeshift shelter. In deference, Drazzle lowered his head. The others did the same.

"We'd best be going," said Drazzle, ending the moment of silence. "The Wanderlust beckons."

Wost smiled. "Sure thing. Around here, we wish travelers the speed of a peregrine falcon. May that, as well as this Wanderlust, take you where you are meant to go."

Chapter 17

Weeks had elapsed since Drazzle and Zeet departed from the Flooded Forest. Over the course of time, Drazzle had noticed the landscape below him was changing. Yes, there were still trees, large and small, and bushes, and meadows of grass, and flowers of numerous colors, and bodies of water, such as streams and lakes, but there were also unmistakable images from Mister Poom's class, Drazzle's teacher back home, which, of course, were originally presented by Q'teel, and his fellow Founders.

Both Q'teel and Mister Poom were graphically descriptive. Beneath Drazzle, he saw familiar places of interest from the time when the Founders were slaves of the Farmers. There were vast, fertile dirt fields, where undisclosed vegetables grew in the soil. Moreover, there were structures, much larger than the beavers' shelters that Drazzle recognized so well. What was the word Q'teel had used to describe them—houses?—yes, that's what they were called. The red one, the biggest building of all, was entitled a barn. Livestock, as they were labeled by the Farmers, dwelled inside. And Drazzle saw those unfortunate beasts, which were big, with black and white patchy markings, in an adjacent pasture. They were confined by an encircled fence. According to Q'teel, the horrible Farmers would take their milk. Sometimes, they would sell them away to be eaten.

The ducks living on the farm weren't exempt from the Farmers' necessities. They would steal their eggs. Even worse, they, too, were used for occasional meals. Eagerly, Drazzle shook his head in desperation to rid himself of these appalling thoughts. The sooner Zeet and he were gone from the countryside, the very territory of the Farmers, the better he'd prefer it.

After all, the irony was not lost on Drazzle. Years ago, the Founders initiated their exodus, encouraged by the wondrous Wanderlust, to start a brand new life elsewhere. Drazzle, under the direction of the Wanderlust revisited, a feeling he trusted, was whisking him away into the past, in a manner of speaking. It was an unusual conduit to find the future.

Chapter 18

Drazzle insisted that Zeet and he clear the farmland as quickly as possible. But this accelerated flight was not without its price. Consequently, both Drazzle and Zeet required a much needed rest. Below, there was a huge, flat green field, which looked smoothed not grassy. Conveniently, this meadow had a pond, which was something that appealed to Drazzle a lot. Indeed, a duck couldn't stay away from the water for very long.

"Let's take a break, Zeet, and land down there. I could use a swim. That, and something to eat." Drazzle proposed.

"Sure thing, no problem. I'm a little hungry, too." Zeet conceded.

Drazzle landed with a horizontal splash on the water. Zeet grounded himself on the edge of the pond. He hopped on the moist sand, and made small footprints, as he searched for something to eat. At last, Zeet found a large, juicy worm, which he plucked from the earth and readily consumed. It was so tasty, Zeet decided to seek another.

Alternatively, Drazzle plunged his head and feasted on some underwater coontail plants. When he reemerged, he heard a hubbub coming from the opposite side of the pond, beyond some capitol pear trees.

"What's all that noise? Sounds like...honking." Zeet said.

"I recognize that language, Zeet. I was taught it in Mr. Poom's class. They're geese!"

Zeet failed to understand Drazzle's excitement. He watched as Drazzle exited the water and proceeded in the direction of the honking. Zeet flew after his friend.

"Drazzle, wait! Where are you going? What's so thrilling about seeing these geese?"

"I'd like to meet them, that's really all. When Wost said he knew of geese living at the Flooded Forest, I wanted to ask him if he'd introduce us, but the hawk attack got in the way. That, and the Wanderlust urged me to move along. This is my second chance to meet my extended family!"

"'Extended family'…?"

After Drazzle and Zeet turned the corner, past the trees, there they were: six geese sitting in a row, engaged in a spirited conversation. One of the geese noticed them and said, hospitably, "Well, hello, brother! Have you, too, come to watch the Swingers?"

Zeet beheld the geese. Yes, there were some similarities shared with Drazzle. They had bills and webbed feet, that much was all true. But these birds were bigger, and their necks were much longer and blacker. In addition, their chests were whitish-brown. Their backs were dark brown. Most noticeably of all were their cheeks, which were marked with a large and curved section of white. Fortunately, the goose addressed Drazzle in Duckish, instead of his esoteric honking; otherwise, Zeet wouldn't have comprehended the greeting.

"You…you called my friend your brother, are you guys actually related?" Zeet inquired.

"You don't see a resemblance? My goodness, and folks think *I'm* a silly goose?"

Laughter erupted among them. Zeet looked at Drazzle, who wasn't participating in the hullabaloo. Evidently, the joke was lost on him, too. Or, in respect to Zeet, he chose not to partake. And soon, after the geese settled down from their revelry, they realized their humor was not embraced, and an explanation was in order.

"You see, my little friend, we're overall fellow waterfowl. Often, my fellows and I have shared comparable shelters, such as lakes and the like. We all fall under the classification of Anatidae. Isn't that a beautiful and impressive word?"

"Yes, I know of you, "Drazzle interposed. "Q'teel and the other Founders spoke of you. They came across your kind during the Grand Pilgrimage."

With astonishment, the goose blinked. "You know Q'teel?"

"I do. I was part of the Colony he established."

The goose turned to his comrades. "The sky isn't as vast as we thought."

He looked back at Drazzle. "I had a grandfather that had met Q'teel. Fondly, he spoke of him. Also, it's really nice to know Q'teel and the others made it to a new home. Evidently, the Wanderlust was as true to him, as he was to it."

"Drazzle's following the Wanderlust, right now." Zeet mentioned.

"Fascinating! Grandfather always appreciated how transcendent Q'teel made traveling sound. As for us, there was nothing all that romantic about it. We simply call it a migration. It's just a way of life for us, coming and going. Speaking of which, have you found your destination yet?"

"No, Sir." Said Drazzle.

"You'll know, I predict, when the time is right. Say, where are my manners? My name is Tream. This is Vark, Flowton, Zay, Meed, and Grite. They're members of my family. And, you are Drazzle, as your cardinal friend called you, yes?"

"That's right, and he's called Zeet."

"Well, Drazzle and Zeet, you are in for a treat! Given the positon of the sun, they'll be here soon!"

Drazzle looked around. "They?"

"The Swingers. Unless, of course, they're prevented by rainfall or wintertime, they're always here. They favor this, the Great Green Expanse, as we've affectionately labeled it."

Flowton said, "Stay and watch them, it's such a lark. They take their long sticks, you see, and they swing them, aiming at a small, perfectly rounded white stone. The object of the game is to deposit that white stone in a hole. The Swingers, they try so hard at accomplishing it. Again, it's such a lark. Join us, you two, and watch the game!"

"Sometimes, we place friendly wagers on the Swingers. We like to pick out our favorites. *Oh*, look! Here they come!" Zay cried.

If Drazzle wasn't already white, he would have blanched from shock. Immediately, he recognized them. After all, Q'teel and the other Founders had described them aptly, *ad nauseam*.

To the geese, they were simply known as Swingers. To Drazzle, they were Farmers!

There they were, dislodging themselves from something which had delivered them. Whatever it was, it had four legs, but they were shaped circularly. The Swingers were featherless, of course, but were dressed in their own layers of protection, comprised of various colors, identified as clothes. Q'teel had taught Drazzle the word. They lugged a cocoon of sorts (that's the shape it loosely reminded Drazzle of, like that of a caterpillar's) that held the sticks Tream had mentioned.

They seemed oblivious to Drazzle and everyone else, as a Farmer/Swinger carefully placed the white stone in position. After being satisfied with its placement, the monster swung its stick and sent the stone hurling into the air, in the opposite direction. According to Drazzle's vantage point, the stone landed quite near the first depositing hole. Apparently, the Farmer/Swinger did well, given his gratified expression. It appeared his comrades were in equal agreement, based on their jubilant voices of approval, and pats on his back. Indeed, this very same energetic endorsement was reflected by the geese, all of whom were cheering.

Again, the players of the Great Green Field ignored the birds. But Drazzle figured this indifference would ultimately become fleeting. In time, they would turn their sights on them and do something horrible!

"Tream," Drazzle said, exasperated. "Do you know what those terrible things are??"

"Is that a rhetorical question, Drazzle? We've already told you of them, they're Swingers."

Drazzle slowly shook his head, nigh offended by Tream's cavalier attitude. "Tream, they're Farmers! If you're aware of Q'teel and the Wanderlust, then you must know them, the reason why the Grand Pilgrimage happened!"

"Yeah," chimed in Zeet. "The ducks left the Farmers to find their independence."

"They're dangerous exploiters! They enslaved my people!" Drazzle insisted.

Tream considered what was said. "Well, in fairness, some of the Swingers could be Farmers, yes. But, as for the dangerous part, the Swingers have never bothered with us before. Now, occasionally, the workers attending to the Great Green Expanse, they've chased us away, this is true. In fact, in an effort to deter our spectatorship, they've even used fake owl statues—there's one over there on the edge of the pond, to your left, do you see it?"

Indeed, they did. The figurine looked rather fearsome. It was a large bird, colored in brown, black, and white. It also had twin horns. Most disconcerting were its big, yellow spherical eyes. Ironically, despite being a faux representation, the eyes looked cunning and alert.

Tream continued to explain. "They think we're gullible. But we're smarter than that. We can tell the difference between the living and the dead. If the Swingers are guilty of anything, it's insulting our intelligence. Now, please, let's have no more distractions. We're missing all the fun."

Drazzle was incredulous. Finally, he said, "Tream, you may be a silly goose, after all. You can't trust them! You shouldn't be anywhere near them! If they catch you, they'll take you away, and then they'll enslave you on their farm! They'll take your eggs from you! They might even *eat* you!!"

With an affronted tone, Tream said, "Well, then, if that's your narrow opinion of our entertainment—and our own common sense—I think you should go. You're spoiling our moods, and our amusement is suffering. Goodbye, *little brother.*"

The way Tream pronounced those final two words stung Drazzle. They felt like an evaluation of his inexperience, a dismissal of his outlander status. Feeling defeated, with no further words to spare, Drazzle simply turned away. He was about to spread his wings and take flight, when Zeet said, "Drazzle, wait. They might be finished with you, but I'm not done with them. Hey, don't you guys just waddle off, not just yet!"

The sharp intonation of the cardinal's voice caused the six larger birds to take pause.

"You know, Drazzle was only trying to help you and keep you safe. There wasn't a need to be so...flippant."

Tream said, "There's also not a reason to treat us as amateurs. We've been living in the 'outside world' longer than you, and we understand how things work. Whatever your past experience, you'd both do well to learn that not all 'Farmers' are the same. Actually, right now, I don't see a difference between them and you. You both underestimate our aptitude."

The geese sauntered away, and followed the Swingers, as they made their way across the Great Green Field Expanse.

"Are you all right, Drazzle?" Zeet asked, sympathetically.

"Yeah, thanks for inquiring. I sincerely hope that they will be, too."

Chapter 19

The next hour was spent silently. Drazzle wasn't in a conversational mood, Zeet had observed, and he chose not to engage him in any small talk. Indeed, he knew it was pointless to try, given how Drazzle had evaded him, when he had first caught the Wanderlust.

Alternatively, Zeet paid attention to the scenery below them. It was beginning to look entirely different from the rural area they had left behind them. There were more dwellings, both bigger and taller, and there were more cars, of all varieties and colors, and more activity. Clearly, they were flying over the terrain of the Farmers, the Swingers, or however you wanted to label them. Beneath them, many of the Farmers/Swingers were busy, living their lives, thankfully oblivious to their aerial transit.

Unexpectedly, Drazzle descended, heading in the direction of another pond, which was nearly as spacious as the one they had visited back at the Great Green Expanse.

"Hey, what's up??" Zeet asked.

Drazzle either didn't hear him, or he ignored the question. In any event, the duck continued to drop away. Finally, he landed smartly on the water and remained adrift in front of quite a spectacle. Zeet pursued him, but stayed aloft, nearby his friend.

"Why'd you leave the sky, Drazzle?"

Drazzle stared at the sight before him. "I've never seen water move like this before. The river at home, it flowed in one direction, and it never danced so energetically. It's beautiful!"

Zeet couldn't contest that assertion. Indeed, this white spray of animated water was a glorious image. In a thinly manner, the stream rose, getting broader as it progressed. It was as tall as a small tree, and, at the top of the vertical stream, the water divided and fell evenly, on both sides, landing prettily on the surface, forming a perfectly white rim. Indeed, so impressed by this display, Drazzle and Zeet failed to notice that they had company.

"Well, well, what have we here?"

The gruffness of the voice snapped them out of the spell the pond fountain had placed them under. Drazzle saw that eight huge water birds had joined him. They had him surrounded in a half circle. The dancing fountain was behind Drazzle, and it served as an obstruction. He could have retreated to the air, but their unexpected advent took him by surprise and temporarily frozen him. Zeet stayed airborne.

One of the water birds said, "Looks to me like trespassers, Captain Pell."

Captain Pell sighed and said, "I know that, Patrick. It was a rhetorical question."

Captain Pell noted Drazzle was looking clueless and determined it was a language barrier, since he was communicating in his own dialect. Accordingly, he switched to Duckish.

"You two don't belong here. This pond, and its land, they're all private property.

"*Oh*, I'm deeply sorry, we honestly had no idea." Drazzle confessed, sincerely.

Evidently, Drazzle's offering of contrition was not accepted, given Captain Pell's stern expression. Ironically, his pale blue eyes blazed with suspicion and contempt. Like Drazzle, he, and his ilk, were entirely white. Unlike Drazzle, his bill was very long. The upper part of it was colored red-orange, while the bottom section was yellow-orange. A patch of yellow-orange encircled his blue eyes. On his head,

Captain Pell had a mane of disheveled feathers. One of Pell's colleagues dipped his big bill in the water. Drazzle saw a fish twitching in the bird's weird throat pouch. Soon, the fish was consumed.

"Well, duck-o, now you do. I strongly suggest that you and your pintsized pal hightail it out of here, or we'll get rough with you."

Zeet snapped, "Pintsized?? Who are you calling....?"

Drazzle felt a pang of *déjà vu*. He thought Captain Pell's bullying attitude was familiar, it reminded him of Druful.

"Zeet, please. We don't want any trouble. In fact, there's something really important I need to tell you."

Captain Pell and his thugs swam closer. "Tell him on your way out of our space. I'm quickly losing patience with you, especially with the tiny loudmouth."

Drazzle said, "P-please, Captain, I'm pleading with you, just l-let me explain..."

"What we got here, mates, is a hearing problem," declared Pell to his peers. "After we're done with him, he's gonna have more than that! Pelicans, attack!"

Drazzle froze with fright. Zeet, still flying, tensed, and was ready to take on these ruffians, despite the fact he was woefully outnumbered and outsized.

"Desist, at once!"

Everyone paused. The pelicans looked toward the shoreline of the pond. As did Drazzle. He saw the source of the shouted command. It had come from a different bird, one which was unknown to him. Another shout was cast to Captain Pell, from afar: "Kindly escort these strangers to me, at once, Captain."

As before, with Pell, Drazzle was incognizant of what was yelled to Pell. Unbeknownst to Drazzle, the language being utilized was Pelicanese. Drazzle watched

Pell closely. For a heartbeat, Captain Pell hesitated. It was clear he still wanted to pummel Drazzle. However, the moment elapsed, and the Captain addressed two of his pelicans. "Patrick and Phillip, you're with me. We'll take these two to the Chief Aide. The rest of you will carry on with your patrols. Get to it!"

The five pelicans dispersed. Pell returned his attention to Drazzle and Zeet. "As for you outsiders, let's move."

Chapter 20

The Chief Aide waited for them on the shoreline of the pond. As Drazzle swam in his direction, with Zeet, flying overhead, Captain Pell and his fellow pelicans followed them.

Before Drazzle reached the dry land ahead, he noticed another perched bird in the shallow section of the water. It had two gangly legs. Indeed, it was nattily perched on one of them. The bird's neck was much lengthier than Tream's, and thinner, too. It had a white/black beak, but the part which oddly curved, like a hook, had the darkest portion. Most interesting of all, the bird's feathers were colored in a jubilant pink. The hue reminded Drazzle of his mother, Vose, because every morning, she would fix a pink lily on her head.

If only she and Drazzle's father, Mez, knew how far he had come. He hoped they were faring well, back home, in the forest. This was a paradoxical time for him to abruptly become homesick. Not now, Drazzle thought.

Drazzle set foot on the sandy ground. Zeet landed next to him. Captain Pell and his cronies stood behind them.

The Chief Aide, obviously astutely instinctive, addressed Drazzle in his native Duckish "Warmest salutations, visitors. I bid you welcome to our home. I am Cyril, the official Chief Aide to our celebrated Potentate, Paresh. It is a pleasure to make your acquaintances."

"Well, now," began Zeet. "That's a better greeting than the one we got from 'Captain Charming'." Zeet turned and glared at Pell, who reciprocated the sour expression.

"*Ah*, yes. You must excuse Captain Pell for his strict approach," said Cyril. "He and his Pelican Phalanx take their duties most earnestly."

The Chief Aide was an impressive-looking bird. Encompassing his attentive yellow eyes was an extensive ruddy splotch, with a slight green streak under his eyes. His feathers were decorative, colored in a dark brown and a bright tan. A pattern of small black diamonds were displayed on his wings. He had a white stripe that encircled his neck. His head was a dark green, and his beak was a pale yellowish tint.

Drazzle said, "I can't begin to share how nice it is to meet you, too, Chief Aide Cyril."

Cyril bowed in a courtly manner. "Dear lad, you've my gratitude. Now, since we've exchanged preliminary pleasantries, it is now time for you to please elucidate on your identities, for it is only proper to know your names, before I conduct my integral interview."

Drazzle took on a curious countenance. "An interview...?"

"Indeed. As Chief Aide, this is one of my responsibilities. What are your names, please?"

"Yes, sure, we'll share, of course. Well, I'm Drazzle Fairfeather. My friend, here, is Zeet Redpebble. We both come from a faraway forest, where a river flows through it, which is home to a Colony of Ducks, my people"

"Yes, but your companion is not a duck."

"That's true, yes. He lived in the same forest, though. We actually made friends with several songbirds."

Drazzle noticed Cyril eyeballing Zeet. For a moment, given the Chief Aide's stare, Drazzle felt peculiarly inconsequential. The Chief Aide then said, shifting his concentration back to Drazzle, "I see. And why, pray tell, Drazzle, did you ever leave your home?"

"The Founder of our Colony, Q'teel, he once caught something called the Wanderlust, a spiritual type of wind that inspires you to leave where you were, and find a new place and start afresh."

From behind, Drazzle heard Captain Pell make a groan of derision. Conversely, Cyril was cautiously curious. He wasn't as dismissive as Pell, and wanted to know more.

"I pay close attention to phraseology, Mr. Fairfeather. You mentioned the word 'caught.' This Wanderlust, it's not contagious, is it?"

Embarrassedly, Drazzle shook his head. "*Oh*, no, Sir, not at all. You know, until now, I never thought about how odd the wording was. I'm sorry for the confusion, but Q'teel's explanation was the way I was taught. I promise, Wanderlust isn't like a cold, or anything."

Cyril considered what was said. "If this were true, how you do account for Mr. Redpebble? I assume he has 'contracted' this Wanderlust, too?"

Zeet chimed in. "The thing you must understand about it, Chief Aide, is Wanderlust is inspirational. If anything, it's spreadable in that manner, I guess. Plus, Drazzle's my best friend, and I didn't want him to go on this journey all alone. I just know, if I stayed behind, I'd miss him, lots. He get me, and I get him."

Affectionately, Drazzle reached out with his wing and patted his little companion. Drazzle knew his father, Mez, was influential in Zeet's accompaniment, as originally admitted by the cardinal, but his passionate words demonstrated a real cognizance of the nature of the Wanderlust. Zeet beamed at him. This was a true friend, indeed. And Drazzle wasn't the only one aware of this display of loyalty.

"How touching." Said Cyril, smiling. "Thank you for particularizing. To be sure, you both seem so genuine.

Moreover, there's discernible potential." Again, Cyril's focus fell on Zeet. To Drazzle, it was unmissable, strangely enough.

"Well, young gentlebirds," the Chief Aide declared. "Your Wanderlust, in its preternatural wisdom, since it has delivered you here, is to be commended. Assuming, of course, this place is your ending destination?"

Drazzle nodded. "It is."

At this, Zeet blinked.

"Very well. I am accordingly convinced you are not threats to our society. Ergo, congratulations are in order, because you have successfully completed the first part of the integral interview.

"That's great, Sir. With whom is the second interview?" Drazzle inquired.

"Why, with Paresh himself, of course! As Chief Aide, one of my functions is to present him new candidates for the Caste of Feathers, the name and system of our celebrated civilization. If he deems you worthy—and I believe you both have promise—you'll be granted placement in our ranks."

Drazzle and Zeet both exchanged inquisitive looks. "Excuse me, Sir, but what does placement mean, exactly?" Drazzle asked.

"If you are accepted, it shall all be explained later. For now, you should concentrate on your second interview. You'll be judged primarily for your appearance, but I do recommend inserting some personality into your appraisal. That, and some deference would be most beneficial. Kindly wait here, please, with Captain Pell, while I go and share my conclusions with Paresh."

"So suddenly? Sir, could Zeet and I have some time to prepare? I mean, we've never met a Potentate before, whatever that is, actually."

The cadence in Cyril's voice changed from enthusiasm to solemnity. "My dear boy, the Caste of Feathers is a closed, yet sophisticated classification ideology. In order to remain here, you must be assessed. Otherwise, Captain Pell will force your departure."

Drazzle turned and saw how much Captain Pell wanted such a result. It was nigh palpable.

"All right, Sir. We are guests, after all. We'll do it your way, of course."

"Splendid! Please, remain here. I will now go to the Posh Palace."

Chapter 21

Captain Pell and his fellow pelicans kept a vigil, with steely, suspicious looks. Drazzle tried to ignore them, as Zeet whispered to him: "I couldn't help from noticing, during the Chief Aide's interview, that you admitted this was your destination. When were you gonna tell me, Drazzle?"

Drazzle answered, "There wasn't really any time. I mean, especially after the pelicans surrounded us. Since then, everything has happened so fast."

"How do know for sure this is the place?"

Drazzle patted his chest. "When we left the forest, I always felt this powerful tugging sensation. It was constantly directing me to somewhere. Along the way of our journey, and all the stopping points, that feeling was constantly there. But, Zeet, the only thing I now feel is a weird absence, kind of like an echo. It's over, the Wanderlust is gone. Q'teel told me about how it felt when the Wanderlust blew itself away from him. Trust me, this is similar to his experience."

Zeet gazed at his friend, as if he was trying to examine Drazzle's soul and confirm the absence of the spiritual wind for himself. Of course, this wasn't feasible, so Zeet had to accept Drazzle's statement. "This is pretty big. Before, I just thought you wanted to see that beautiful display of dancing water."

"No, there was more significance in my landing here than that."

Captain Pell said, "Look alive, you two. The Chief Aide is back."

Indeed, Cyril had returned. He announced, "I have Paresh's permission to introduce you to him. Follow me, please, gentlebirds."

Chapter 22

The Chief Aide guided Drazzle and Zeet up a hill. Behind them, Captain Pell and his soldiers followed. Zeet hitched a ride on Drazzle's back, as he waddled upwards. While in transit, Zeet looked around. He saw many birds just going about their daily business. One of them was bobbing its head and pecking the ground, and she was making a clucking sound, while doing it. Drazzle recognized her as a hen, which was another bird that was enslaved by the Farmers. Q'teel had mentioned them in his stories.

Zeet also recognized a gaggle of geese, Tream's people, waddling and chatting with each other. There were even ducks, but none of them were white, like his best friend.

"The Wanderlust must've have delivered you to the right place, Drazzle. I mean, it matches what you told me in your daydreams. Look at all these different birds for you to see and meet. It's basically what you had described."

"Yes, definitely. I noticed that, too."

Zeet chuckled, puckishly. "Also, don't forget the other thing you mentioned."

"What's that?"

"Meeting someone important. You know, like a girlfriend...?"

As before, when this topic was broached, Drazzle's cheeks became a bright pink.

"Well, you gotta admit, it's a possibility, given the way things are going."

Drazzle didn't respond. The embarrassed tone of pink hadn't faded. Subsequently, Zeet decided to change the subject.

"So, what's your take on this Caste thing?"

"I don't have a clue. I've never heard of it. I'm certain we'll know more about it soon enough."

Zeet pecked at his wing, a means to take care of an itch. "No doubt. Did you happen to notice the Chief Aide was gawking at me, as if I were a juicy strawberry to be eaten?"

"I did. It was weird, all right. I don't have an explanation for that, either. One thing is for sure, they don't believe in letting the grass grow under their feet. We're about to meet their Potentate, the most important bird of this Caste system."

There was something else that Drazzle couldn't avoid from wondering about, and it was the big structure at the top of the hill, which was coming into view. It was all becoming too familiar. After all, in graphic detail, Q'teel had described these buildings in his stories. Indeed, in the distance, flanking the building, were fences, wide and high. Drazzle wasn't thrilled with this sight at all. Could the Farmers have a presence here? And, if so, why?? What would be there connection to this Caste? Unless, the Caste exists on a farmland!

Cyril stopped short, a minor distance away from their destination. "I'll remind you, you'll be judged mostly by your exteriors. During the process, be respectful. By doing so, it could profit you. I trust that you both understand?"

"Kind of, yes," said Drazzle, although, the intonation in his voice suggested an anxious, indeterminate awareness.

"Very good. Paresh awaits!"

Cyril led them to the structure known as the Posh Palace. It was rather enormous, and designed like a dome. Its walls were light grey, and it had six windows, which were shaped liked rectangles. The surface of the windows were smooth and created a shimmering effect, which made it was impossible to perceive what was within from the outside. The roof was black and globular. There was a doorway, fringed by two Phalanx pelicans. Seemingly, this was the only entrance to the fortress. The Palace also had a great balcony, which partly stretched across the spacious pond, an ideal vantage point to view the water below and the fenced in landscape. Again, this particular architecture resembled the achievement of the infamous Farmers. Seeing it up close, it gave Drazzle an uneasy feeling.

Protruding from the Posh Palace, from above the ingress, was a long, gray ledge, with an iconic spiral-shaped edge. Lying leisurely on it was Paresh.

Chapter 23

Involuntarily, Drazzle stared. He simply couldn't help himself. Paresh was undeniably a spectacle.

Paresh's iridescent feathers were blue, a more ostentatious shade than that of the sky. He was also comprised of a glitzy green, which distinctly outshone the color of the grass. If a Potentate was considered to be royalty, then his crown—if that's the right word for it?—appeared to be a small tuft of flowers, comprised of the same flashy hue of his shimmering blue neck. If they were actually flowers, could that signify Paresh was not completely a bird and was partially plant? Drazzle pushed away that silly thought. Undoubtedly, he was a vision, though, and the drab grey that consisted of the ledge beneath him made his loud mystique unavoidably noticeable.

The pheasant called Cyril proclaimed, "I beseech you, O Connoisseur of Chroma, our Coordinator of Caste Assignment, our Specialist on Style, our beloved Potentate, Paresh, may I present Drazzle Fairfeather and Zeet Redpebble! While we await your acknowledgement, we shall gratefully bask in your irresistible incandescence"

Upon completion of his vibrant verbosity, Cyril genuflected. For a few seconds, since they were unaccustomed to such a ceremony, Drazzle and Zeet stood stationary. From behind, Pell made a not-so-subtle *ahem* sound, and, having taken this as a cue, they soon followed Cyril's example.

With attentive eyes, Paresh looked down on them. Quickly, Paresh rose to his feet. "You may all rise.

Newcomers, stand apart. I require an appropriate radius for my appraisal. I shall begin with the duck."

They did as they were instructed. Even Cyril stepped back. Gingerly, Paresh leaped from the ledge. Drazzle quickly understood the request for a reasonable ambit. Paresh had a long train of decorative feathers that flowed from him, which were blue, green, and turquoise. Unnervingly, those lengthy plumes held numerous oval-shaped eyes. Maybe this was why he was competent evaluating others, he had an uncannily pervasive sight. If so, though, why were they behind Paresh? Drazzle figured, nobody could ever sneak up on him. Paresh spoke with an exotic accent, which accentuated his vividness, and his voice suggested he was from a faraway land, much like Drazzle, except he felt he lacked the Potentate's physical pizzazz.

Suddenly remembering Cyril's advice, he thought it would be proper to say something: "We're very pleased to meet you, sir."

Paresh ignored him. Methodically, he circled Drazzle, whom, by the way, was beginning to feel nervous, being on display, as he was. Paresh started talking, but it dawned on Drazzle, the Potentate was 'thinking out loud.'

"He's almost pristinely white, yet there are subtle tinges of yellow...yes, I can envision a sultry summer's day, and this one took refuge under an outsized sunflower. Due to the temperature, he reposed, and also due to the balminess, the yellow petals above him 'melted' and trickled and bonded to his paleness."

Of course, none of this extravagant dialogue was remotely true, but Paresh was clearly enthused by his own magniloquence. His talent for storytelling was unmistakable.

Paresh stopped circling Drazzle and announced, "I do not have a duck of your description. Thus, Mr. Fairfeather, I shall decree a Tier be added for you."

Before Drazzle could ask what a Tier was, the gaily-colored bird turned away from him and shifted his attention to Zeet. Evidently, Drazzle's assessment was over.

With a similar verve that Cyril had exhibited, Paresh looked at Zeet with a keen interest. As the former did with Drazzle, the latter circled the cardinal, and made comments to himself.

"And this one, a vision in vermillion, he is extraordinarily blazing with exuberance. I love the crest, a most contemporary coiffure. His ebony masque, it is decidedly chic. Yes, this one is a must-have. I need an addition of red, indeed. Accordingly, I will add a Tier for you, Mr. Redpebble."

Theatrically, suddenly, Paresh pivoted, which startled both Drazzle and Zeet, as Drazzle jumped back, and Zeet dodged, to avoid his ornamental train.

"Cyril, I want you to assemble everyone at once. We must have an official ceremony for these two new additions, and to explain and reconfigure the Caste."

Cyril said, while he bowed, "Consider this done, Your Excellency." Cyril hurriedly went away.

"Captain Pell," said Paresh. "Escort this pair to the Caste Pyramid. As for me, I must prepare myself to address my ardent audience."

With no further words, Paresh disappeared through the doorway of the Posh Palace and disappeared.

Drazzle looked at Zeet, and the small, red bird seemed as flummoxed as he felt. Captain Pell flapped his wing forward, and said, rather grumpily, "Follow me."

It was observable to Drazzle, Pell didn't agree with Paresh's decision to let him and Zeet stay. Drazzle and Zeet started walking, shadowed by Pell's Phalanx soldiers.

Chapter 24

This was the second major celebration that pertained to Drazzle. When Q'teel proposed a going away bash for him, Drazzle was embarrassed. After all, since he wasn't very popular back at the Colony, his attendance for his birthday parties was lacking. It was overwhelming to have everyone assemble for him, for his big sendoff to follow the Wanderlust.

Drazzle never considered the possibility of such hoopla ever occurring again for him. But, that's exactly what was happening. Whatever this Caste of Feathers precisely was, they were coming to welcome him, and, of course, Zeet.

Drazzle took it all in. Cyril wasted no time in gathering the rest of the Caste. There were some familiar birds, such as the geese that resembled Tream and his kind. There were other geese, but they were entirely white, except for orange bills and legs. They kind of reminded Drazzle of himself, only they were larger. Drazzle also saw other ducks, but, they, too, differed from him. Some of them had bright green heads, and their bills were yellow. They also had a white ring at the base of their necks. Moreover, they had brown counterparts, but they were feminine in nature.

Drazzle saw more clucking birds. As they walked, they bobbed their heads. They had red combs atop their heads and wattles that dangled beneath their chins. These hens came in different colors, such as brown, black, and white.

Besides the hens, there were other familiar sights, such the roosters, male chickens, which were bigger than the ladies. Their combs, which were as red as Zeet himself, were even larger than theirs.

"Say, Drazzle, look, there're robins, blue jays, and goldfinches!" But...I don't see any cardinals." Zeet said.

Sure enough, there were none. Manifestly, these other aforementioned birds were members of the Caste. So far, Zeet was the only of his kind to be present. This struck Drazzle as a curiosity, as he reflected back on how Paresh and Cyril had taken such a special interest in his friend. Being new himself, Drazzle didn't want to engage in any dubious speculation. Perhaps the other cardinals were simply tardy and that was all. Then, a new thought occurred to the duck: Cyril seemed too fastidious, too thorough, to brook lateness, so maybe there was another explanation to consider.

This conjecture was fleeting, because Drazzle became distracted with the arrival of the second strangest bird, after Paresh, of course, he had, to date, ever encountered! Zeet must have felt similarly since he never commented on the absence of other cardinals.

She walked on reedy and long legs. Her neck was also lengthy, and she had a bill that was bent. She was slender in form, and had her flight feathers, which were black, on the ends of her wings. What made her stand out so dramatically was her pink plumage. When Drazzle first arrived, he only saw her from afar, but seeing her up-close, that was something else. Again, the bird's pink pigmentation reminded him of his cherished mother, Vose.

Another standout was the curvaceous arrival of another member of the Caste. Respectfully, she was big, and clearly, a water bird, all white, except for her orange bill. On this bill, there was a black 'inkblot' splotch and knob. Most prominent about her was her neck, which was long and S-shaped. She spoke not a word. Her form communicated an air of elegance about her. Drazzle felt, with the other ducks, and geese, and this one, there was an abundance of Anatidae.

Aside from these 'relatives', the sight of the blue jays caused Drazzle to think of his father, Mez, the Colony's Director of the Division of Defense. Mez was stern but his love for this son was unimpeachable. The blue jays worked closely with the Division, and would warn the Colony if any foes were approaching the river. Drazzle wondered what type of function the jays served in the Caste.

In the back of this Caste assemblage, Drazzle noticed a group of birds, all of whom were mostly dark brown in plumage. Mostly, because, in those feathers, there was a shimmering russet-green. The males, in comparison to the females, were larger and had spurs of lengthy beards on their chests. Both genders had wattles, which were reddish. Given their body language, they presented a lowly, unwanted aspect.

All the birds in the Caste were grouped in their own species, with the exception of Cyril, whom, incidentally, there were no other pheasants and he was standing next to a schematic of a pyramid, made up of neatly arranged pebbles, at the base of the towering tree. Drazzle saw there were spaces between these rows, which was convenient for new add-ons, he thought to himself. Not far away from the pheasant, there was a pile of pebbles. Paresh was nowhere to be found, though.

Until...

The roosters Drazzle recognized from before had starting crowing, in unison, which really spooked Drazzle and Zeet, because it was all unanticipated and resounding. On a metal barrel, partly entrenched in the ground, they danced and created a dynamic drumming sound.

Drazzle and Zeet couldn't believe their eyes. They both should have anticipated a splashy entrance from Paresh, but they weren't expecting this one at all!

Paresh was dancing to the continuously disseminated rhythmic *cock-a-doodle-doo* sounds of the roosters. And he was hardly boogying alone. Beside him was a facsimile, who was definitely feminine, but lacked the overall brilliance of Paresh's color scheme, as her feathers were less loud, and more of a creamy hue. The only hint of color that resembled Paresh was her gleaming green neck. Atop her head was a cluster of flowers, her crown of a sort. She also did not have the protracted tail of Paresh. Nonetheless, they uniquely and pleasingly juxtaposed.

Together, they moved with a flawless choreography, as if they were poetry in motion. They twirled, they leaped, they kicked, and they wiggled. The female was so nimble, she would effortlessly jump whenever Paresh spun his tail feathers. The audience wasn't content to sit still, they reacted with cheers and applause. Well, most of them, anyway. Drazzle saw one brown duck, who was struggling to feign excitement. Moreover, he took notice of the birds in the back of the assembly, whom, incidentally, were putting up a façade of enthusiasm. Captain Pell himself looked as grim as ever, too.

Finally, the roosters stopped trumpeting, and the energetic dancing came to a climax. Paresh and his partner stood there motionless, in the perfect pose of a grand finale. The ovation became louder. The two performers took it all in.

Drazzle was getting the notion that this 'welcome to the Caste of Feathers' formality was more about Paresh and his lady. He was feeling secondary.

The female dancer took her place in front of the audience. Paresh went and stood next to Cyril. With an extended wing, Paresh signaled the Caste to hush, and they did.

"Thank you, one and all, for the very warm reception. My wife, Prisha, and I, are quite flattered.

And now, it is time to increase our Caste of Feathers. It is time to add more Tiers to our magnificent Pyramid of Configuration."

Chapter 25

The Caste was silent, insofar as, one could have heard an acorn plummet to the ground. With bated breath, they awaited Paresh to speak. As hosts, Drazzle quietly compared and contrasted Paresh to Q'teel. The Chief Founder loved to throw, in the word of his choice, a shindig, and he knew how to hold the concentration of his spectators. But, as a master of ceremony, he never made the event about himself. He was dedicated to the source of the celebration. Conversely, Paresh craved the limelight. He liked being the center of attention. Q'teel would pause to stoke up the exhilaration, but it was a fleeting effect, whereas Paresh only did it to prolong being the hub of the moment. It was tortuous to Drazzle and Zeet, he was certain of, how the Potentate would leave them in suspense.

"As deemed by my steadfast expertise in all matters of perception and refinement, I shall add a Tier for this sole duck, Drazzle Fairfeather. Come forth and be known, Mr. Fairfeather."

Drazzle approached the Potentate. The nervousness he first felt back at his going away party had reasserted itself. At least, then, it made better sense. The Wanderlust had chosen him, after years of being gone, and that was something worthwhile for the Colony to express joy. His admittance to the Caste seemed trivial and superficial. After all, he was judged primarily based on his looks. He was about to learn more about Paresh's initial assessment of him.

"Because of your aesthetics, those subtle tinges of yellow, you will go above the Tier of the White Geese. Subsequently, this characteristic of yours, which is absent in them, you'll be able to dine before them. However, similarly to them, you may not dwell in the Posh Palace. That privilege goes to my chosen entourage, the most picturesque members of the Caste."

Drazzle saw Cyril bow. Undoubtedly, the Chief Aide was allowed inside Paresh's home.

"Cyril, kindly make a change to the Pyramid of Configuration."

Upon Paresh's command, Cyril walked to the pile of pebbles and used his beak to carefully extract a few. Next, he sensibly situated them horizontally in the empty spaces between the pre-established Tiers. Cyril took a step back and admired his work. The Caste applauded.

Paresh said, "Mr. Fairfeather, you will now take your place between the Tier of the Swan, and the Tier of the White Geese."

Drazzle was rooted to the spot. He looked at Zeet, who was looking correspondingly confused.

"Take your place, *now*." Paresh ordered, with a tone of insistence. Drazzle was then snapped back to reality, and he waddled past Zeet, and past the other Tiers, to his declared destination.

"Mr. Redpebble," Paresh proclaimed. "Step forward and be known."

Zeet hopped to Paresh. Drazzle witnessed how Paresh seemed to be more enthusiastic about Zeet's addition to the Caste. It was the same vim Paresh and Cyril had demonstrated once before.

"Because of your vigorous vermillion aesthetic, I shall assign you your own Tier. It will go between the Tier of Pelicans and the Flamingo Tier."

Zeet looked at the pink bird. Whether she was upset about being bumped down a level was unclear, since she didn't show any disappointment. For the first time,

Captain Pell acted amused. It was evident from the start he didn't care for Zeet, or Drazzle, for that matter, so being overtly recognized in the Caste as someone superior pleased the pelican.

"I now decree, Mr. Redpebble, you will dine after the Phalanx and before the Tier of the Flamingo. Moreover, you will be granted access to the Posh Palace."

"Now, just wait a berry-picking minute! Are you saying, I can live in your fancy home, but Drazzle, my best friend in the entire world, can't?"

Paresh looked both astonished and affronted. Apparently, he wasn't accustomed to being interrupted. Cyril, as the Chief Aide, quickly stepped in to his Potentate's defense.

Cyril spoke politely, gently, due to the fact the cardinal held some level of significance, yet Drazzle noted an undercurrent of condescension in the pheasant's voice.

"Mr. Redpebble, since you are a neophyte here, we shall overlook your impertinence. At least, this once. Paresh cleverly established your Tier because of your feathered exterior. He has determined your value in the Caste. You, my little friend, should be rejoicing, not carping. His judgment has propelled your status. Ergo, it would be impossible for Mr. Fairfeather to share your Tier with you. Your caliber is incompatible."

Zeet was flabbergasted. Before he could retort, Cyril continued to explain: "Take heart, though. You are free to interact with one another. The Caste of Feathers isn't strict in that fashion. However, there are certain social obligations you must obey. Do you comprehend what I am telling you?"

Zeet's beak was about to open, when, from his vantage point, Drazzle exclaimed, "Zeet, it's all right!

Remember, we're new here, and we've got to get used to how things are done here!"

Paresh looked infuriated. As Drazzle deduced, he didn't like the loss of the limelight. Captain Pell sternly yelled, "No more outbursts! We'll have decorum—or else!"

Cyril was more diplomatic. "Bravo, Mr. Fairfeather. That's the correct attitude to embrace. With time, you'll assimilate to our customs."

"Indubitably" said Paresh, having taken control of the situation. "You will both discover that my rules are astutely designed to evoke order for our fabulous society. If you adhere to them, you will serve as facets of something truly unique. However, I will caution you: if you somehow fail to comply, if you deviate, I will force you into exile. And your journey here would all be for naught. Now, wouldn't *that* be a shame?"

Silently, Drazzle nodded. Zeet mutely raged, but offered no further protests.

"Splendid. I accept your commitment to the Caste of Feathers. Should you have any questions, you may call on my Chief Aide, or Captain Pell and his Phalanx, or, as Cyril indicated, any other members of our eclectic assemblage. Gradually, you'll learn about our laws and customs. Two things you must know immediately: first, my word is gospel. Second, your rank in Caste affords you some authority. A bird beneath your Tier should show deference and obey instructions. The same, of course, goes for someone above your Tier. Now, in the meantime, since it is Sunday, the Caretakers will be serving breakfast in an hour. I suggest we prepare for that. This induction ceremony is over."

Who were the Caretakers, Drazzle contemplated? Furthermore, what was a Sunday? And why was that brown duck, the one who was pretending to revel in Paresh's earlier performance, bashfully trying not to look in his direction?

Chapter 26

Paresh had concluded the orientation event. The birds of the Caste were dispersing.

Unfortunately, Drazzle had lost sight of the brown duck, the one who was looking at him. She waddled away and disappeared into the crowd.

Zeet was beside himself. "Can you believe that dumb rule of Paresh's? Just because I've got red feathers, and you don't, I can live inside the Posh Palace, but you can't! It doesn't make any sense to me!"

"It's...peculiar, I know." Replied Drazzle.

"That's all you've got to say? You know, you shouldn't have interrupted me. I wanted them to know how I felt about things."

"Everyone knows how you felt about things, Zeet. You made your feelings on the matter quite plain."

Zeet crossed his wings. "Well, if they think I would live in that place of Paresh's, he's gonna be sorely disappointed. I mean, it's not fair. You're my best friend. It would be totally wrong, being separated from you like that. I just can't believe you took a stupid policy such as his so calmly."

"We need answers. And I think I know a possible means of getting them."

Captain Pell approached them. "All right, you're both part of the Caste. Just make sure to fly straight from now on. I won't tolerate any more temper tantrums from you both like I saw earlier; am I making myself perfectly clear?"

Drazzle, knowing full well Zeet's fiery mood, used his wing to shield the cardinal, a means to quell him.

"You needn't worry about us, Captain Pell. We perfectly understand you."

Captain Pell's yellow eyes narrowed. With a rigid gaze, he scrutinized the duck for a beat, and then went away.

Drazzle removed his wing from Zeet. "Why'd you stop me, Drazzle?? I wanted to give that overgrown talking pouch a piece of my mind!"

"We really can't afford to antagonize someone who already has it clearly in for us, Zeet. Paresh encouraged us to ask questions, to learn about the Caste, and I think there's someone here capable of doing that. I just need to find her."

Zeet's anger subsided. It was replaced with intrigue. "She?" he asked.

"Yes. Paresh said we've an hour before breakfast will be served by these mysterious Caretakers. Let's make good use of our time. Come on."

The terrain of the Caste was immense. At least, it seemed this way to Drazzle, who was still learning about his new home as he made his way across the grassy land. Moreover, the duck assumed Zeet felt similarly, given his own size. This place seemed to be its own world, within an outside world. Surely, the fence prescribed that belief. One section of this place was comprised of the Potentate's Posh Palace, and its balcony. And, of course, there was the capacious pond, and the sandy shore it touched. There was a profusion of trees, flowers, and bushes, too. Beyond the vast encompassing fence, there was a small green forest.

Finally, she came into view. She was reposed, at the base of a cluster of purple alliums, which grew at the edge of the Westside of the lattice barrier. Her eyes were closed tightly, and she was unmindful to Drazzle and Zeet's presence.

Drazzle beheld her. It was as if a charitable tree bestowed a boon upon her and colored her in its various tints and shades of brown. Her orange bill was speckled in brown. On her wing, outlined in white, was a brilliant stripe of blue. Incontestably, she was beautiful. She was also a teenager.

"Is this the one you were looking for, Drazzle?" asked Zeet.

Abruptly, her eyes opened. "Excuse me, but may I ask why you are both staring at me?"

The unmissable irritated tone of her voice had shaken Drazzle, which caused him to lose his own. His awkwardness had seized him in this inopportune time, especially when he wanted to express himself the most.

Zeet sensed his plight and took the initiative. "Hi, my friend, here, his name is Drazzle. And I'm Zeet. But, you already know all this, because you attended our introduction party shortly ago, and, for some reason, Drazzle wants to talk to you about something. Isn't that right, Drazzle?"

Although, Drazzle knew Zeet was only trying to assist him, he swiftly felt mortified. She was looking so suspicious and perplexed. Drazzle knew he had to salvage the situation, and quickly.

"Yes, Zeet, you're totally right. Say, I was wondering, could you please excuse us for a moment? Why don't you go and explore our new home, okay?"

Zeet looked at Drazzle, and then, at her. There was a flash in his eyes, a revelation of cognizance, and he said, with a wink, "I take your meaning. Consider me gone."

Zeet flew away. Impatiently, the girl asked, "What do want from me?"

Drazzle said, "I'm glad you can understand me. I know many of you are already acquainted with Duckish, and…"

"Duckish and Mallardarian aren't all that different. The linguistics are fairly similar."

"Thanks for clarifying."

Silently, she was staring holes into him. Clearly, she anticipated a reason why they were even talking.

Drazzle again addressed her. "I'm sorry to have interrupted your nap, I…"

"*Oh*, I wasn't sleeping. I was actually meditating."

Drazzle confessed, "I've never heard that word before, what does it mean?"

"It's a technique that helps me to calm my nerves. In my mind, I visualize things that make me happy, and…" she trailed off, as a look of embarrassment had seized her. Then she said, as she rose to her feet. "But, yes, you *did* interrupt me. I think I'll leave."

Drazzle beseechingly extended a wing. "Please, don't go. I'm very sorry for disturbing you. I…I just want to talk to you."

"Why?"

"It's because…well…I noticed you didn't seem interested at all in Paresh's glitzy entrance. Also, *uh*, I saw you trying not to make eye contact with me, and…"

She unexpectedly looked worried. "You discerned that? If you did, one of the others could have, too."

Drazzle waddled closer. "No, please, be calm. I honestly don't think anyone else paid attention."

She sighed. "I sincerely hope not."

"Why were you worried about the others' reactions?"

"Look, I don't know. As such, I'm not comfortable discussing anything with you."

She again started to go, when Drazzle said, "I don't blame you for being guarded. Basically, I am a stranger. Aside from Zeet, I don't have any friends in the Caste. I'd like to make one."

She turned around. "Well, I can certainly relate. I don't have any, either." Her tone matched her forlorn expression. "And what caused you to think I have the potential for friendship?"

"I don't know for sure, I'm just hoping you'd be willing to give it a try."

She seemed confounded. "I'm not used to being noticed. Not like this, anyway."

Her words were honest. Drazzle said, rather genuinely, "I'm actually surprised to learn this. If you ask me, you've an agreeable presence."

She smiled. In spite of herself, she couldn't help it, Drazzle perceived.

"Could I ask you your name?"

Intrinsically, she debated. Visibly, she was dithering. Eventually, she said, "I'm Delta."

Delta. It carried a resonance, a pleasant one, to Drazzle.

"It's really nice to meet you, Delta. I've never heard such a name before. It's very unique."

"As is yours. It sounds indicative of a distant clime."

Drazzle loved her parlance, she sounded so intelligent. In her, he sensed a kindred spirit, an outcast, misunderstood here among the Caste, as he had been, in the Colony.

"That's because I am from somewhere else," Drazzle admitted, "But you already knew that."

She nodded. "Yes, of course. Whatever brought you here, of all places?"

He detected some sullenness in her voice, especially pertaining to the last three words of her sentence.

"If you like, I'll share my story with you, Delta."

Again, she nodded, her way of granting consent.

Chapter 27

While Drazzle was busy, Zeet decided to meet up with three of the little members in the Caste. There was a goldfinch, whose feathers were made up of bright and cheerful yellow. The robin had a bright orange underbelly, which contrasted well with the gray-brown plumes his body. The blue jay was a perky blue, with accents of white and black features.

They were chatting amongst themselves, and Zeet landed right next them.

"Hello, everyone! How's it going?"

The goldfinch answered, "We're doing great. How are you?"

"The same, in fact. Thanks for asking." Zeet replied. "What are your names?"

"I'm Grat," answered the goldfinch. "The robin's name is Rriss, and the blue jay is called Bazz."

"Nice to make your acquaintances. So, how long have you guys been in the Caste?"

Bazz said, "For months, really."

"I see. Tell me, then, do you actually agree with Paresh's crazy rules? I mean, don't you think it's kind of ridiculous that not everyone can live in his home, as big as it is?"

"You'd do well, Zeet, to not blurt out such opinions. They'll only get you into trouble. And why ruin a good thing such as this?" tweeted Rriss.

"A good thing? What do you mean?"

"Well, the free food, for starters." Grat shared. "It's preferable to seeking nourishment, in the wild, where danger lurks."

97

"And don't sneer at the Posh Palace, either." Chimed in Bazz. "It's warm and safe. And the pelicans keep out the riffraff."

"The riffraff?" Zeet said, with disgust in his voice. "You just insulted my best friend!"

Bazz ignored Zeet and continued to talk. "Sure, the ones in the Caste the Potentate has deemed unworthy. But that's something you don't have to worry about, Zeet. Your red feathers have earned you a better status than most, exactly like our colors did for us."

"Yeah, speaking of my red feathers, Bazz, just where are the other cardinals? I mean, surely, there must others."

Bazz looked at Zeet, as if he was a simpleton. "Weren't you paying attention? Paresh assigned to you your very own Tier. There are no other cardinals."

"Why is that, though?"

Rriss interjected with, "The weather has been lovely recently, hasn't it?"

"Ideally balmy, yes, I agree." Said Grat.

"Come on, fellas, it seems like you're sidelining me. Besides, given my color and rank, don't you have to answer me?"

Zeet didn't really want to impose his will on them, because it felt distasteful, but he was feeling desperate.

Grat said, warningly, "Since you're slow at taking hints, Zeet, I'll be brusque. That particular topic is forbidden. In fact, it's against the law to talk about it. As such, that supersedes your request."

Unintentionally, Zeet took a step back. He was taken aback by the piquant assertiveness of the goldfinch's voice, which contracted his seemingly sunny disposition.

Rriss cheerfully said, in an effort to change the subject, "May I propose a new topic? What did you all think of Paresh's performance earlier? Wasn't it amazing?"

Zeet was thunderstruck. He couldn't care less about that. What concerned him more was their dedication to deliberate obscurity.

Chapter 28

Delta was an attentive audience.

"That was quite a tale."

Drazzle shared, "Thanks for listening, I do appreciate it."

She nodded. Drazzle could tell she was prudently processing his story. It was a lot to take in, indeed.

Ultimately, she said, "Is it possible the Wanderlust made a mistake?"

Drazzle was taken by surprise. "Why would you say that?"

Before she could reply, another duck appeared. It was another mallard, but he had a bright green head.

"There you are, Delta. I knew I'd find you here, with the alliums, your favorite spot. Breakfast will soon be served, you know."

"I know, Meridian. But, what's the point in arriving early? There's a pecking order, and my turn won't come up for a while."

Meridian said, "I know. I just wanted to check on you, is all."

"Thank you. You needn't worry, I'll be along soon enough. I'm getting acquainted with our latest Caste member."

Soundlessly, Meridian scrutinized Drazzle. It was pretty intense. Then, he simply said, "See you soon, then."

Meridian left. As if Delta could read his mind, she expounded on Meridian's connection to her. "He's my brother."

"*Oh*, okay." Drazzle felt some relief wash over him. "Should we make our way to the eating place? We can talk as we go."

"Do you even know where we eat, Drazzle?"

Since they started talking, it was the first time she said his name. It made his heart beat faster. "Not really."

"The Zookeeper will provide the food outside the Posh Palace."

As much as he wanted to know what a Zookeeper was, he had a more important question to ask.

They waddled, side by side, through the grassy floor as they made their way towards the Posh Palace. Strangely, he felt an urge to reach his wing out to hers, but he quickly suppressed it. Where was this bravery coming from, he thought to himself? Perhaps becoming a seasoned traveler had made him pluckier."

"Delta", he finally said aloud, "why were you concerned about the others noticing you?"

Delta frowned. "Paresh expects participation from his subjects. Fortunately, since I'm practically invisible to most, my disinterest is ignored. If this changes, I could get in trouble."

"What does 'trouble' mean? What would happen?"

"In general, the Pelican Phalanx pays more attention to you. That's something I'd rather not contend with, really."

Drazzle entirely understood that anxiety. In a short amount of time, Zeet and he were already cast in that unwanted spotlight.

"What do they do, exactly?"

"They intimidate you until your behavior improves."

"And if it doesn't improve?"

She shuddered. "You lose your place in the Caste. You are forced into exile."

When they drew closer to the Posh Palace, Drazzle saw that the birds of the Caste of Feathers were again organized in their respective Tiers. Zeet was present, too. For some reason, he looked chiefly vexed. Of course, Paresh and Prisha were front and center. They all patiently waited for the Caretakers to show themselves.

There were five large bowls placed in a horizontal row: turquoise, emerald, magenta, orange, and yellow.

The Caste needn't wait any longer, for two creatures had emerged from a door originally unnoticed by Drazzle.

They were tall and thin, yet they were strong, because they hefted various large bags each. These entities were featherless, peachy in flesh tones, all dressed in beige uniforms. They both wore safari hats, which shaded their faces. They seemed to be women, based on how they were once described by Q'teel, back on the farm.

Drazzle's blood ran cold. The Caretakers were Farmers!

Chapter 29

Stupefied, Drazzle could only watch. His thoughts were lost in a convoluted labyrinth.

His fears were actualized. Paresh's Posh Palace, the fence that surrounded the home of the Caste, they all pointed to the handiwork of the Farmers.

Carefully, they each unzipped their own bag and poured its contents into a respective bowl. From his viewpoint, Drazzle saw chopped greens, corn, and pellets fall into the turquoise bowl. In the magenta bowl, fell dried shrimp, carrots, and red peppers. The emerald bowl contained meal worms, pellets, and wax worms. Inside the orange bowl held corn, seeds, lettuce, and oats. The red bowl housed thread herring.

After they finished pouring, the Caretakers cheerfully beckoned the birds to come forward, to accept their contributions, but the Caste held back.

Drazzle helplessly watched as the Farmers disappeared through their secret side panel doorway into the Posh Palace. Drazzle looked at Zeet, who had a countenance of sheer stupefaction. Drazzle finally realized Delta was no longer by his side. She had returned to her own Tier. Drazzle was the only bird that was out of the Pyramid formation.

Cyril approached him and said, "Remember where you belong, Mr. Fairfeather. Go there now, *please*."

Still in a state of shock, Drazzle made his way to his spot, directly between the Canada and the white geese. He desperately wanted to talk to Zeet, but he was closer to the front of the Pyramid. Drazzle also wished he could speak to

Delta, but she was looking straight ahead. It wasn't surprising, given what she had revealed to him.

Cyril announced, "As always, as the pinnacle members of our Pyramid, the Potentate and his charming wife shall first feast."

Drazzle quickly decided it was asinine to watch Paresh and Prisha eat. The turquoise bowl was theirs. They both took their sweet time, while everyone had to wait their turn. It was no wonder, then, why Delta was in no hurry to arrive any earlier. Drazzle deduced that particular bowls were for specific birds, which made the waiting period even more frustrating. Eventually, they would be accessed, but only in the customary sequence set by the Potentate.

Finally, after Cyril, Captain Pell, and some of his Phalanx pelicans (some were still on duty, patrolling, Drazzle saw, from afar) had a chance to eat, it was Zeet's turn. Being new, Cyril directed him to the emerald bowl. Zeet flew up and landed on the rim of the bowl. Before he dipped his head to eat, he turned around and addressed Paresh personally, with an entreaty.

"Look, Mister Potentate, Drazzle and I always have breakfast together. And there's plenty of food available, so why can't he join me up here?"

Paresh looked distraught. It was the same expression he displayed once before. Obviously, he wasn't accustomed to such disruptions to his supposedly flawless social system.

Captain Pell stepped forward. The pelican was perturbed. "I told you before, pipsqueak…!"

Paresh composed himself and then whispered something to Cyril, and then, the pheasant interjected, "There's no need to lose one's temper, Captain Pell. After all, the lad is a tyro. He simply needs another reminder about our societal procedures, and..."

"Actually, I don't. It's totally fine. I'll...I'll play along. I'm...sorry." Zeet said.

Drazzle was surprised Zeet relented so easily, as were Cyril and Paresh, and even Pell, for that matter. Zeet started to eat. Drazzle wished he could know what Delta was thinking, but she kept her back turned to him. She appeared stoical. She was playing it safe.

"Is it possible the Wanderlust made a mistake?"

Those words, recently spoken by Delta, echoed in his mind. Drazzle himself once wondered if the Wanderlust had misguidedly chosen him, but Q'teel assured him otherwise. It blew him here, over a considerable distance, as he traversed the sky. Despite the increasing evidence, this was no time for him to lose his faith in the Wanderlust's wisdom. Coming here couldn't have been a mistake. Conceding that would mean this was all for nothing.

"Is it possible the Wanderlust made a mistake?"

"No," Drazzle whispered to himself. "There has to be a reason why I was sent here."

A goose from behind Drazzle had cleared his throat, and when Drazzle turned around, the goose was giving him a peculiar gaze. The goose must have overheard Drazzle talking to himself.

Drazzle suppressed his twinge of embarrassment and focused on what was really important. He needed answers, and he felt that Delta was his most viable source.

But he knew he had an obstacle to overcome: Zeet.

Chapter 30

The turkeys were the last to partake in breakfast.

Drazzle actually felt sorry for them. There were a lot of mouths to feed in the Caste, and, by the time it was even his turn, much of it was consumed. Moreover, some of the bowls, such as the pink one, for example, had specific food inside, which was for the flamingo known as Florida.

It saddened Drazzle to see the turkeys move so pokily to the red bowl, with no enthusiasm whatsoever.

After the turkeys finished, Cyril made an announced that the Visitors would be arriving in the next hour.

Paresh, Prisha, and Cyril entered the Posh Palace, while Captain Pell addressed some of his Phalanx soldiers, whom, incidentally, were in a circle, engaged in a covert conversation.

The rest of the Caste were going their separate ways and carrying on with their morning.

Drazzle and Zeet met up. "We really need to talk, Drazzle," said Zeet.

Drazzle nodded. "We do, yes. But not here. Let's go by that part of the pond's edge. It's currently unoccupied."

When they made it to the proposed place, Zeet didn't hesitate to say, "We've got to go, right now!"

"I was prepared for this. I figured you out. You thought arguing was moot, because we weren't going to be around here for much longer. It's the only reason why you yielded so easily earlier about not sharing breakfast together."

"Exactly right!"

Drazzle started to walk away from Zeet. "I'm sorry, but leaving isn't an option for me."

Once more, Zeet took flight and landed in front of the duck, which caused him to halt.

"You can't be seriously considering staying here! You saw those two Farmers! This place isn't safe at all! And don't get me started on this crazy Caste thing! It's just a trivial clique!"

Drazzle said nothing. He just braced himself for what was coming next. And he was correct, for the cardinal continued his argument.

"I really hate to say this, I truly do, but I think the Wanderlust goofed. Maybe your version of it was faulty, or worn-out. Why else would it take us *to* a farm—yes, Drazzle, that's what this place is—a farm, and we just tried to disregard the clues because we so wanted to believe in something bigger than us! We must now face some hard facts, something has gone horribly wrong."

Silently, Drazzle processed his best friend's words. This was the second time someone had suggested this postulation. Then, when he spoke, he did so in a calm tone of voice. "Zeet, weren't you the one who said this environment matched my daydreams? Didn't you admit that the Wanderlust had delivered us to the right place?"

"Yeah, well, I didn't have all the answers yet, now, did I?"

"And we still don't. But Delta could help us with that."

"Whom?"

"She's the mallard I met, before breakfast. You know, back at the alliums."

Zeet's dismay somewhat subsided. "*Oh*, she's the reason why you want to stay, isn't it?"

Drazzle said, with the same composure, "Partially, yes. I'm going to be honest with you, as you were with me, Zeet. Yes, I'm very scared to be here. I'm fighting the urge to run away. All my life, I was taught about the dreaded Farmers. Do I want to end up as dinner for them? Of course not. Yet, there's something that frightens me even more than they do. As you already know, I gave up everything to invest my time and soul into the Wanderlust. As did you, for that matter. If I believe we weren't meant to come here, if I accept defeat and fly away, I think that would be a more tragic fate than any other."

Again, Zeet had considered how far his friend had come, both in distance, and in character. He was deeply moved by Drazzle's commitment to the Wanderlust. It may have left him, but Drazzle remained devoted to it. Could he do no less? Plus, there was something else he couldn't discount. Something he even teased Drazzle about, actually.

"You told me about the possibility of meeting someone important, Drazzle, when you reached your new home. So far, things have been adding up. Despite my fears, I'm going to stand by you, because I care about you a lot. Having said that, let's go and find Delta." Zeet said.

With tears in his eyes, Drazzle lovingly scooped up his little companion and embraced him.

"Thank you, my dear friend," said Drazzle.

Chapter 31

Drazzle and Zeet quickly found Delta.

It wasn't hard, since she had returned to her favorite spot, her patch of alliums.

As before, she was meditating. Her eyes were closed. She looked peaceful.

This time, Drazzle wouldn't be 'creepy' and addressed her at once. "Delta?"

Delta's eyes opened at once. "You're still here? I'm actually surprised. To be honest, after you told me your story, I'm amazed you made it through breakfast. I know how much the Caretakers—our name for your Farmers—frighten you."

Drazzle said, "They still do, really. That hasn't changed. Nevertheless, there...there are things Zeet and I must know, though. First of many, what exactly *is* this place??"

Delta looked to her left, and then to her right, while she spread her wings, a presenting gesture, while saying, "It's called a zoo."

Zeet cocked his head. "Never heard of that. Is it another name for a farm?"

"There's a small farm here, Zeet, but that's only a facet of the zoo, which, of itself, is more elaborate. Essentially, it's a public park, comprised of various animals, for the Visitors to come and see us all."

Drazzle enquired. "Visitors?"

"Yes, they're the same as the Caretakers, only the latter are officially affiliated with the zoo. By now, the zoo should be open, and the Visitors will be along soon."

Zeet and Drazzle shared scared facial expressions. "There are more of them coming??" Zeet asked.

"I assure you, there's nothing to fear from them."

Drazzle said, "Delta, I told you about how they treated Q'teel and the others. They're selfish monsters!"

Delta shook her head. "Maybe the ones they knew were dubious, but our Caretakers look after us. They feed us, they keep us safe and healthy. In fact, do you see that hen over there?

"I do."

The hen was strutting and pecking the grassy ground. Using her feet, she kicked away some dirt. Her feathers were a bright caramel color.

"Her name is Butterscotch. Once, she was sick. Subsequently, a Caretaker took her away. In a few days, she was returned to the Caste, right as rain."

It was Drazzle's turn to be an attentive audience. Even Zeet was quiet, as they both absorbed her words. She spoke so convincingly, it was almost hard to believe this was the same bashful and dejected mallard he had recently met.

"You see, without the Visitors, the zoo wouldn't exist. We wouldn't have a home, and no there wouldn't be any Caretakers to watch over us. To us, they are everything."

Drazzle gave it all plenty of practical thought. He suddenly remembered the birds he had met along the journey. There was Wost and Strattonash, totally unlike, yet they formed a friendship. Tream and his kind, they weren't afraid of the Swingers, their name for the Farmers, and Tream tried to impart on Drazzle that these featherless creatures weren't identical in nature. These were the lessons they shared with him, and Delta was giving him another perspective. Maybe, just maybe, not all the

'Farmers' were wicked. Maybe it was unfair to clump them into one category. Still, for Zeet's sake, and Delta's, and, of course, his own, he wouldn't dare lower his guard.

"If you wish," Delta said, thereby ending Drazzle's silent contemplation, "I could give you a tour of the zoo."

"You're allowed to leave the habitat, Delta?"

"*Oh*, yes. Even before Paresh's arrival, we were considered to be the privileged ones. We're permitted to roam beyond the fence."

Drazzle felt confusion. "Why, then, does the fence even exist?"

"For our safety, of course. Also, it defines our section of the zoo. If you like, I could give you a tour of the outside."

Without hesitation, Drazzle declined. "No, thank you. I don't think I'm ready for such a step. Besides, I think I need to learn more the Caste. Speaking of which, could I ask a question?"

"Go ahead."

Drazzle's serious expression matched his tone of voice. "Why do you think the Wanderlust made a mistake?"

Her confidence abruptly faded. Her despondency had reasserted itself. She lowered her head and shared, "It's because, Drazzle, this habitat used to be so different. It's a shame you didn't come sooner."

Drazzle came a little closer. "You said something about Paresh's arrival. That's when things changed, didn't they? Will you please tell me about it?"

She lifted her head. "Come with me, I need to show you something."

Chapter 32

Delta guided them back to the section of the habitat where the balcony protruded over the land below it.

As Delta predicted, some Visitors had appeared on the balcony. The more muscular one, with a bearded face, lifted his child and placed her on his broad shoulders, so she could get a better view of some of the Caste members that were present. The female, an adult, like the male, clutched the railing and leaned over. She was interested in the white swan called Concerto, who was drifting serenely on the pond's surface. These featherless Visitors also took noticed of Florida, the pink flamingo, who was balanced on a single reedy leg in the shallow part of the pond, near its shore. They also reacted to a gaggle of white geese, all of whom were in transit to the water.

As interesting as these aforementioned birds were to the Visitors, they were quickly upstaged by Paresh's arrival.

But this entrance was different from his prior one. Paresh was sans his wife, and there wasn't any music, nor backup dancers.

Instead, Paresh sashayed, as his long train of his feathers, slowly and meticulously, spread in a fan formation, an arc of extravagant green and blue eyes...dozens of them...were unblinking.

Indeed, Drazzle was almost hypnotized by Paresh's lurid exhibitionism. It was both surreal and disconcerting. Drazzle looked at Zeet, who was equally mesmerized. Even the geese stopped in their tracks to view the peacock.

Evidently, the Visitors on the balcony were impressed with Paresh, especially their little one, who was pointing and cheering at him. The woman held something in her hand, and she aimed it at Paresh. It flashed a few times, like lightning. Occasionally, the peacock would pause and pose for her. He's obviously received this recognition before, as he basked in their attention.

The bearded male tossed down seeds he had secured from a dispenser on the balcony.

The nearby geese didn't go for the seeds, which Paresh gleefully ate, knowing they were exclusively his.

Drazzle and Zeet were spellbound, until Delta's sobering whisper ended their transfixed state. "He acts more like an entertainer than a leader." Her words were emphasized with resentment. "Before the zoo closes, Paresh will perform several more times."

Drazzle whispered back to her, "I can't deny it, Paresh is extraordinary. But what was the point of watching him?"

"*Ah*, you see how easily you were taken with him. That's how he took control of the habitat. As I said, the Visitors are important to us, and Paresh became important to them, and that's exactly how he exploited our connection to them."

Drazzle did indeed understand the glamor; however, only to an extent. He watched the Visitors, from a highpoint, while they observed Paresh eating his seeds. It was weird, this voyeurism. Drazzle wanted to know more. No longer whispering, he said, entreatingly, "Tell me everything."

It would be naught, though.

Delta's brother, Meridian, intervened.

Chapter 33

Meridian said, in a definitive voice, "That's enough, Delta. I want you to come with me, right now."

Delta was confused, as were Drazzle and Zeet.

"Meridian, is there something wrong?" asked Delta.

Meridian ignored her. Instead, he spoke directly to Drazzle and Zeet. "I think it would be best if you both left my sister alone. She already deals with enough anxiety and depression and she doesn't need additional stress from the likes of you."

His words struck Drazzle like a physical blow. He was hurt by this harsh assessment. Drazzle looked at Zeet, who was clearly angered, but the cardinal held his tongue. After their latest conversation, Drazzle suspected Zeet didn't want to further exasperate the tension of this moment.

Delta herself was muddled. She didn't comprehend why Meridian was doing this.

"M-may I ask why you're feeling this way, Meridian?" Drazzle inquired.

Compared to Drazzle, the mallard was smaller in stature, but Meridian's vehemence unmistakably made up for the size difference. Meridian came closer to Drazzle. "I thought I just explained myself to you."

Zeet's ire was increasing, yet he silently restrained himself. However, Drazzle spoke up. "With respect, Meridian, in a short amount of time, I've grown...fond...of your sister, and I would never want to upset her. I think she could use a friend. Aside from you, Delta shared that no one else pays attention to her, and..."

Meridian interjected. "It's...nice...you want to befriend her, but I would have preferred someone less...controversial."

Meridian talked to Delta. "The Phalanx have taken notice of these two, Delta. You've seen it for yourself. We don't need that kind of unwanted attention, and if you continue to associate with them, it's going to end badly." Meridian jerked his head in Paresh's direction, whom had finished his seeds, and was already flouncing for a new audience of Visitors. "We don't want him to notice, either."

Zeet finally talked, but it wasn't the eruption Drazzle had expected. He communicated with composure. "Look, don't fault Drazzle for my actions. I'm the hothead, he isn't. He's a good duck. And, I know this will sound nutty, but we were brought here by very special circumstances. Maybe helping your sister is the reason for it all. Delta knows our story, tell your brother, Delta, won't you?"

Surprisingly, Delta didn't respond. She seemed defeated. Initially, she had said she wanted to avoid undue surveillance, and Meridian had reminded her. Gently, he placed a wing on her shoulder and led her away.

"I'm so sorry, Drazzle. I tried to help. I sincerely did."

Drazzle nodded, as he helplessly watched Delta leave. She looked back him. Her eyes were watery, with regret.

Chapter 34

Life in the Caste took some getting used to.

If not for Zeet, Drazzle would be companionless. The other members of the Caste were civil, yet not overly friendly. Perhaps the reason for this was why Meridian preferred that Delta wouldn't associate with him: he was deemed controversial.

Zeet wasn't too keen on socializing with the other smaller birds, especially after the way he was recently treated.

Another observation Drazzle made about the others was they favored their own company. The white geese were constantly grouped together as were the turkeys, the mallards, et cetera. Cyril once remarked, "Birds of a feather flock together." Maybe this proverb made it simpler for Paresh to form the Pyramid's Tiers. He just arranged them according to their appearances.

Zeet suggested a reconnaissance of the zoo. Drazzle rejected the idea, because he feared for his little friend. After all, the place was teeming with Visitors, whom, despite Delta's assurances they were benevolent, Drazzle couldn't entirely trust them. Zeet argued, since he was small, he would be perfect to explore what was beyond the habitat's fences. Reluctantly, Drazzle acquiesced.

And whenever Drazzle was close to being in Delta's orbit, Meridian would briskly escort her away. Or, if he wasn't available, she would excuse herself from the possibility of interacting with Drazzle. Once, Drazzle had tried to approach her at the purple alliums, but she promptly flew away. Drazzle considered pursuing her, yet he decided to respect her desire for privacy. After all, she was avoiding him for the sake of self-preservation.

Consequently, Drazzle did his best to maintain a low profile. However, he found this to be challenging.

Often, he saw things in the Caste that didn't meet his approval.

One night, there was a wind storm. Subsequently, some tree branches were broken and fell to the ground. That morning, the turkeys were clearing away the debris. They would snatch the twigs with their beaks and take them to a designated spot, in a faraway corner on the south side of the habitat, where they dwelled. One of the turkeys, a male, moved pokily, not merely because he was large, but due to his old age. The senior bird did his best to keep up with his younger peers, even though it was obvious he was struggling.

Drazzle approached the old timer and said, "Please, sir, let me help you."

The turkey looked staggered and released his branch. It simply wasn't a matter of being offered assistance, it was deeper than that, Drazzle sensed. It was because he wasn't accustomed to being addressed respectfully, or even at all.

Even the other turkeys paused and were fascinated by the young duck's altruism.

Using his bill, Drazzle started to drag the broken branch. The elder turkey recovered from his stupefaction and aided Drazzle.

The hen, Butterscotch, saw what was happening, and said to Drazzle, "*Oh*, honey, you don't have to do this. It's *their* job."

Drazzle stopped and said, "With respect, ma'am, is there any harm in helping someone with an assigned job, or otherwise?"

Butterscotch gave him a derisible look. "As Untouchables, menial work is their duty. You're on a higher Tier, so doing this degrades you."

Drazzle winced inside. He didn't care for this word 'Untouchables'. "I think it's more degrading to think of another person as less. I also think it's disrespectful to treat an elder this way."

The hen abruptly looked abashed. She began to walk away. However, she stopped and turned and regarded Drazzle. She then moved along.

"Let's keep going, sir," said Drazzle.

The turkey spoke slowly, in a deep voice. "No, son. Go on with your day, before you get in trouble."

Drazzle followed the turkey's gaze and saw that one of Captain Pell's pelicans was watching. He didn't look happy.

The turkey spoke again. "We're not worth the bother, young one. After all, we're nothing."

Drazzle was rendered speechless. All he could do was watch, as the turkey resumed his task.

The pelican stood motionless and stared proverbial holes into Drazzle.

For yielding so readily to intimidation, Drazzle felt absolutely ashamed.

Then, there was the matter with the grey squirrel.

One afternoon, Drazzle was sauntering along, until he heard a commotion.

He saw a pelican angrily flapping his wings in pursuit of the squirrel. Expertly, the small, furry one climbed the fence and stopped at the top, and heatedly chittered away at the Phalanx soldier.

Drazzle was familiar with the squirrel's language, because he knew of them, as they were denizens of his former forest home. He heard the squirrel saying, "You've no right to keep me from my nut!"

The pelican snapped, "I've got plenty of right, 'cause this here's private property. You were trespassing!"

"But I buried my nut long before you made that rule! It's not as if you'll be taking advantage of it. Besides, you birdies never cared about us squirrels being on your land in the past!"

"Well, fuzzy-tail, that was then, and this is now, ain't it? Whether we use it or not, the nut belongs to the Caste, and that's all there is to it! So scram!"

"You truly are a dirty bird!" said the squirrel, as he crawled down the fence and scurried away.

Drazzle thought to himself, where was the harm in simply letting the squirrel take his food? It just seemed unnecessarily mean to deny him.

The pelican realized Drazzle was watching and shouted, "No rubbernecking, you! Now, move along!"

One time, Drazzle overheard a rooster and hen, two expecting parents, talking.

The hen said, "I hope our children will be beautiful."

The rooster nodded, as he said, "Me, too. The more colorful their feathers are, the better their rank will be in the Caste."

The hen looked at her wing, which was feathered black. "Yes. With any luck, they'll be on a higher Tier in the Pyramid than I. I want better for them. They deserve it."

"I agree, my wife. They should have a better social status, like I do. With any luck at all, they'll have my greens and golds in their plumage."

Drazzle could hardly believe his ears. Even he was surprised when the words poured out. "Isn't it more important that your chicks are born healthy? And, no offense, ma'am, but I don't see anything wrong with you. You really shouldn't uphold this dismal opinion of yourself."

The pair were startled by this eavesdropper's outlook. Drazzle expected the robust rooster to peck him into oblivion, but he was rooted to the spot. He and his wife locked in glances, mutually shameful ones.

And then, there was the invitation.

"*Ah*, there you are, Mister Fairfeather!"

"*Uh*, hello, Chief Aide. What may I do for you?" asked Drazzle, who was swimming in the pond.

From the shore, Cyril beckoned Drazzle to approach him. "I've an invitation to extend to you, lad. You, and your confidant, Mr. Redpebble. Where, pray tell, is he, Mr. Fairfeather? I see him not."

"Right now, he's taking a tour of the zoo."

The Chief Aide said, "How nice. You do know you could have accompanied him, do you not? After all, as the privileged ones, we may leave the habitat for saunters and such."

"'The privileged ones, sir?"

"Indeed. The Caretakers favor us. Since many of us are able to fly over the fence, they don't deter us. Speaking of that, it's really why I have sought you. The zoo is now closed, and as a special coda, the Potentate hosts an event called Poetry on the Tortoise. Come with me, please."

Drazzle shook his head. "Thank you, sir, but I really shouldn't. To be honest, I expected Zeet to return by now, and I think I should wait for him."

With regret, the pheasant smiled. "*Alas*, we've no time to wait for his return. The Potentate himself requested your presence. However, this invitation is mandatory. Paresh will be disappointed Mr. Redpebble isn't available, but there's always the next recital, I suppose. Now, kindly follow me."

Since a veto wasn't an option, Drazzle reluctantly trailed Cyril to the fence, and together, they flew over it. They didn't go away too far from the Caste's territory. Cyril led Drazzle to a habitat nearby. This time, there was no fence to bypass, just a waterless moat. Again, the two birds took flight and entered the creature's dwelling.

There was Paresh, of course. Proudly, he stood on something somewhat familiar. Something Drazzle recognized from the river that resembled a turtle, but this one was much bigger! Cyril called it a tortoise, Drazzle recalled. Paresh was stood on its huge shell, which was covered by a patchwork pattern. The tortoise's skin was greyish-green. It had bulky, scaly legs. The reptile ate a head of lettuce, utterly unheeding to Paresh's presence, and his audience, whom were made up of Canada geese, white geese, mallards, and hens. Strangely, there was no sign of any pelicans. Delta was present, with her brother, Meridian. Somehow, seeing her here, made Drazzle feel a little better, even though his thoughts were on Zeet. Where was he??

Paresh warmly said, "Thank you for coming. And now, for your entertainment, I shall begin":

I am your illustrious and exquisite Potentate
Becoming yours was indeed glorious fate.
I am decidedly handsomeness incarnate
I evaluate all colors, turquoise and scarlet
I designed a Caste system, a perfect one
You loyally obey, and my will is aptly done
You are cognizant of my tremendous aesthetic
Undeniably, my charisma is phenomenally magnetic
I am Paresh, your heaven-sent answer to life
During my effervescent reign, I banish all strife

Drazzle suffered through that poem, and more of them. Whenever Paresh finished, there was applause. Cyril would yell out words like "encore" and "author" which overwhelmed Drazzle, because the poetry was so bad. It was all about the peacock's narcissism!

Often, Drazzle looked at Delta, who appeared attentive, but Drazzle knew better. She was playing along, for her own safety. Even her brother, Meridian, put up a good front, but Drazzle saw through that façade, too.

Clearly, he was bored, too. The other members of the Caste were harder to read. Drazzle hoped Delta would look his way, yet she never did.

Drazzle kept expecting Zeet to show up, but this never happened. Hopefully, by the time this awful recital was over, and Drazzle returned to the Caste's habitat, he'd find his best friend waiting for him, safe and sound. Drazzle was feeling very regretful for not accompanying the cardinal, because, maybe, if he got in trouble, he could have helped to rescue him. Drazzle would not forgive himself if some ominous fate ever befell Zeet.

Chapter 35

Drazzle was elated when he saw Zeet back at the habitat. The sun had set, and numerous stars twinkled against a dark canvas.

Paresh and his chosen few had retired inside the Posh Palace. The rest of the Caste went to their preferred nighttime spots to slumber.

Only some of the pelicans stayed awake, as they patrolled the perimeter of the habitation.

"Where were you?" Zeet chirped.

"Don't ask, just be glad you weren't there for it. Where have you been?? I was so worried about you!'

Zeet looked back in the direction of the fence. "This zoo is enormous, especially for a bird of my size, Drazzle. Where we're standing, right now, is just a section of it. There's so much!"

Drazzle's curiosity took over him. "Tell me what you saw!"

"Well, the place's teeming with these Caretakers and Visitors. As Delta said, they look after the needs of the creatures here. And, speaking of creatures, there are so many of them! All sizes, all different kinds of things, you couldn't imagine everything I saw!"

Drazzle's eyes enlarged. "Tell me more, please."

Zeet continued. "These other beings, despite their differences, they've all one thing in common, they're confined."

"Confined?"

"Yeah, either behind glass, or dry moats, or bars."

Drazzle couldn't grasp the reason for such a fate. "Why is this so? Are...are they prisoners? Did they do something wrong??"

"I don't know. What I've gathered, Drazzle, is they're all on display for the Visitors, like the Caste."

"That does support what Delta told me, that this zoo exists solely for the Visitors. Why they would come only to goggle at helpless creatures, well, that goes beyond me. I mean, it seems so mortifying. I know Delta believes in these Caretakers, but I'm not entirely convinced they mean well. They're just another version of the Farmers, if you ask me."

Zeet hopped closer to Drazzle. "Funny you mentioned a farm, 'cause the zoo has one, too."

"Delta said as much, I knew of it, Zeet."

"Well, Drazzle, I spoke to some sparrows and they told me about the farm, which has its own hens and roosters. The sparrows told me they're not crazy about the Caste at all, which they don't agree with Paresh's politics. However, if proven to be sincere, they've taken in defectors from the Caste."

Drazzle pondered what information his friend provided. "That's very interesting, Zeet. It's pretty clear that Delta is miserable. Now, I'm not thrilled about a farm, but if it's a better alternative than this place, why not take it?"

"Maybe her brother won't let her."

"Maybe. He does have an amount of influence over her, yes. Did you ask the sparrows why they weren't members of the Caste? Did you ask them why there weren't any cardinals?"

"I did. They said they weren't interested in joining. There were other means to find food in the zoo. As for the cardinal question, they said they didn't know. I believed them."

Silently, Drazzle nodded.

"Look, I want to bring something up," Zeet said, in a careful, yet cogent tone. "We've got a place to go. We don't have to stay here and deal with this Caste crap. We could relocate to the farm. Who knows, maybe the Wanderlust wanted us to go there, all along."

An irony, thought Drazzle, to consider living on a farm. "No. I can't leave. Not yet, anyway. Delta said this habitat was different. And that difference started with Paresh. Under these horrible circumstances he's made, there's got to be a reason why Delta stays here. I need to understand why. "

Frantically, Zeet waved his wings, in a halting movement, and said, "Have you forgotten Meridian? He said to keep away from her."

"I'm sorry, but I can't let him stop me. I must know what happened here. In the morning, I'm going to talk to her."

Zeet grinned. He was inspired by Drazzle's renewed dynamism.

Zeet said, "We'll both go and talk to her, Drazzle."

Chapter 36

That morning, Drazzle and Zeet found Delta. She was swimming in the pond.

Meridian was nowhere in view. Nonetheless, Delta wasn't alone.

Other mallards in her *sord* were with her. One, in particular, was shouting snobbish taunts.

The female mallard yelled, "You think you're better than all of us. You think you're smarter than any of us. But guess what: Nobody wants you around. When you hang out by yourself, you're actually doing us all a favor."

Zeet, in midair, above Drazzle, said, "Somebody's picking on Delta!"

Drazzle felt *déjà vu*. This bully, Drazzle thought, must be the equivalent to his own, which was Druful. And, much like Druful, this one had her own cadre of toadies. Drazzle also took notice of a Phalanx pelican nearby on the shore, but he acted uninterested. He was more engrossed in grooming himself. Apparently, taking action against this mistreatment of a Caste member was beneath him.

"Yes, I see, Zeet. And I'm putting a stop to it!"

Zeet watched his friend briskly waddle to the pond and swim to Delta's side. The main tormentor, and her fellow mallards, were surprised by Drazzle's sudden arrival. And, for that matter, so was Delta, whose bill was gaping.

Drazzle said directly to the bully, "Have you ever considered how hurtful your words can be? You should be ashamed of yourself—all of you, in fact—for being unkind to a fellow duck! Now, why don't you do us a favor and leave us alone!"

The bully was rendered speechless. She didn't like having her own paraphrased words hurled back at her. Meanly, the other mallards giggled. The bully felt mortified and tried to regain momentum when she said, glowering, and "Well, well, well. If it isn't everyone's latest topic. You should show more respect to me. I'm on a higher Tier than yours."

The other girls stopped chortling and looked smug. The bully won back their respect.

Without a warning, from above, Meridian swooped down and landed on the water, in a skidding motion.

"And my Tier is above yours, Vanessa. So, shove off." Meridian said.

Vanessa sported a sarcastic smile at Meridian, and then she started to go. The girls quickly followed her.

Suspiciously, Meridian looked at Delta, as he asked, "What's *he* doing here?"

Zeet, while flying overhead, in a circle, said, "For your information, Drazzle stopped them from bothering Delta."

Meridian looked at Delta, who was nodding wordlessly her confirmation of Zeet's announcement.

Meridian stood next to Delta. He said, "Thanks for what you did, but it doesn't change anything. I still don't want you to be near my sister. Delta, let's go, right now."

"No." Delta said, simply.

Meridian pivoted. "Don't sass me, Delta!"

Delta moved away from her brother, towards Drazzle. "You're wrong, Meridian, when you said Drazzle's actions don't change anything. It changes everything for me. I know you're trying to look after me and protect me, but it's finally time for me to make decisions for myself."

Delta looked Drazzle directly in the eyes. "Drazzle, when we first met, I was meditating. I told you I would visualize things that made happy. And what was the reason for this? It's because I'm miserable. Don't act surprised, Meridian, you know this. The fact of the matter is, I don't recognize the people here any longer. It hurts me, badly. In order to make me better, I picture how life was before Paresh arrived. It was better, then."

"Delta, stop talking!" Meridian snapped.

Delta ignored him and persisted. "You probably think what I said was paradoxical, especially given the fact I'm immaterial to so many. But it's the truth, Drazzle."

Delta reached out her wingtips to Drazzle and he reciprocated. "I was wrong to tell you the Wanderlust made a mistake. If anyone erred, it was I. You approached me in friendship, yet I rejected you. I was more concerned about the status quo. It prevented from me from accepting you. And that's when I had a revelation. I realized I don't want to live in a society where I'm afraid to be friends with someone. You've made a difference in my life, Drazzle. And if the Wanderlust sent you to do only that, then your journey was successful."

Drazzle's cheeks turned fuchsia, a brighter tint than Zeet had ever noticed displayed by his friend. Zeet, like his best friend, was very moved by Delta's words. And they were hardly the only ones.

Meridian said, "I think I made a mistake, too. I'm...ashamed...to admit it, but, after breakfast, Captain Pell came to me. He explained how Drazzle was a troublemaker, and if I truly cared for you, Delta, I should steer you away from him. Captain Pell said Drazzle would drag you down with him. And...I hate to say it...based on what I saw, I had to agree. You were making major ripples, Drazzle. But you obviously did something else...you made a positive impression on sister. I...I think I was wrong to keep you apart."

Lovingly, Delta hugged Meridian. "Thank you, Meridian."

Zeet landed on Drazzle's head and said, "Why would a jerk like Captain Pell worry so much about Drazzle?"

Drazzle quickly added, "Yes, I was wondering that, too. I'm no threat to him, I'm just a simple forest duck."

Delta released her brother. "*Oh*, no, you're not. You're more than that. As Meridian said, you made ripples. It hasn't gone unnoticed, especially by the birds that favor the existing state of affairs."

Drazzle said, earnestly, "Please, tell me the origin of the Caste."

"Not here. Let's take flight, beyond the fence, inside the zoo. I know a place."

Meridian stood in front of her. "Now, just a moment, Delta. I'll relax a little about you being friends with these two, but you still gotta be careful. The Phalanx are obviously paying attention to Drazzle and Zeet, and we can't afford unwanted trouble in our lives."

"I think we've already crossed a line, Meridian. If they're watching, then they know you didn't take Captain Pell's advice. I'll admit it, I'm scared. This is risky, to be sure. But Drazzle deserves to know the truth."

Drazzle said, "Couldn't the Phalanx follow us to wherever we're going?"

Delta spread her wings. "The pelicans never leave the habitat. We'll be all right. Come on, let's go."

Chapter 36

Delta guided them to a place away from the Caste of the Feathers, away from the watchful eyes of the Phalanx of Pelicans.

It was a place that had several picnic tables, all colored in a dark green, a mossy hue, and a large pavilion, of the same shade, which stood in close propinquity. Also, nearby, there was a playground. In the background, a forest could be seen.

"The Visitors like to eat here, it's called a picnic area. And their children, they like to play on the slides and swings. When we were old enough to fly, our parents would take us here. Gleefully, the Visitors would throw us bread to eat. Do you remember, Meridian?"

"I could never forget it, Delta. It's a happy memory," said Meridian, sentimentally.

"I've yet to meet your parents, Delta," commented Drazzle.

"I'm afraid you won't be able to, Drazzle. They're gone."

Drazzle and Zeet lowered their heads, simultaneously.

"I'm so sorry, "came from Zeet, genuinely.

"You've my deepest condolences, both of you." Drazzle said, sympathetically.

Delta shook her head and said, "*Oh*, I didn't mean it in that sense. What I meant was, they were transferred by the Caretakers to another zoo. Thank you, though, nevertheless."

"You...you don't know where they are? If...if they're...okay?"

"No, we don't. But we choose to believe they are exactly that. And I can already hear your thoughts, Drazzle. You're thinking: 'How could you let something like that happen? These so-called Caretakers that we trust so implicitly, they can do whatever they wish with us, just like a Farmer would.'"

Drazzle was indeed speechless. He was thinking precisely what Delta had articulated aloud.

Delta said, calmly, "Being transferred to a different zoo is just another aspect of zoo life. Think of it as a version of your Wanderlust, this being sent away. Your own parents let you go to face the unknown, didn't they? We did something similar."

In a sense, that was true. At least, the part about facing the unknown. But Drazzle had his parents' consent to leave. In the zoo, there seemed to be a glaring absence of permission. Instead of arguing the differential, because he didn't want to make the siblings feel badly, Drazzle opted to learn the answers he was really seeking.

"That's how Paresh arrived here, wasn't it? He was transferred from a different zoo."

Delta nodded, and her countenance seemed to reflect compunction. "Yes."

Delta left the sidewalk and stepped onto the grass. The others followed. As she sauntered around the playground, she talked. "Once, we were known as the Community. Everyone was equal, then. The Posh Palace was simply a sanctuary, shared by all. When the Caretakers fed us, there wasn't a dining regulation. Things were simpler. That was, of course, until the arrival of Paresh, and his wife, Prisha. Many members of our Community were instantly taken in with them, especially Paresh. After all, none of us had ever seen peacocks before. The novelty was potent."

They walked around what was called a sandbox. Protruding from the sand was a small blue pail, with a red shovel.

"Sorry to ask, but were you also immediately intrigued with Paresh, Delta?" Drazzle asked.

Delta flinched. Her body language was answer enough, but she still said, "Yes. I felt the allure. And so did you. It's the very reason why I wanted you to see Paresh perform for the Visitors. I needed you to see what he was capable of, Drazzle."

"I can't deny it, Delta, I was impressed." Drazzle conceded.

"I was, too." Zeet admitted.

They all went closer to the slide. Zeet bypassed the ladder and flew to its top and slid obliquely down the winding chute. Zeet hopped off and landed on the sand below. "That was kind of fun."

"The Visitors' little ones seem to enjoy it. And speaking of the Visitors, they weren't exempt from Paresh's splendor. He dazzled them, as he did us, on his official debut at the zoo."

"Let me guess," said Drazzle. "Paresh spread his train. He performed for an unsuspecting audience. Everyone was captivated."

"In an instant, Paresh's popularity increased substantially. Being an opportunist, he quickly realized how much the Caretakers and the Visitors meant to us. Billing himself an expert on beauty, colors, and refinement, he proposed he could restructure the Community. He insisted he could usher in a new order and make things better. Easily, he won support, because he cajoled Cyril, Florida, Concerto, and others.

Drazzle said, "Which, I'm gathering, was accomplished effortlessly, because he obviously had the approval of the Visitors/Caretakers, and he used that codependency against you all."

With a webbed foot, Delta kicked a small rock away. It was pretty clear to Drazzle she wasn't happy with the assertion of 'codependency', and that gesture was an example. "Please, don't degrade our relationship with them. They've given us food, shelter, and they keep us safe. They mean so much to us, when we're hatched, our parents let *them* name us. Don't speak ill of them, please."

For a moment, an uncomfortable silence ensued. Meridian ended it by saying, "Tell 'em about the peacock feather, Delta."

"Once, when Paresh was on a saunter, outside the habitat, one of his feathers must have disconnected, which is a common occurrence for us all. But this random moment became more significant. You see, a Canada goose, whom had left our ground, for a walk of her own, witnessed a Visitor, a male, one of whom had picked up that discarded peacock feather, and he gave it to a female, his mate, it seemed, whom, incidentally, was visibly touched by the gift. When that goose returned, she told the story and it spread as fast as a lightning bolt. It only served to further Paresh's prominence to the others. He next declared himself a Potentate, and he started his assessments of us and then arranged everyone into Tiers."

"And the Caste of Feathers was born." Drazzle said, disgusted.

"Yes. In order to enforce the Caste, Paresh brokered a deal with the pelicans. In exchange for their service, they would be given a higher Tier. They enjoyed their new roles and the power that accompanied them. They became gruff bullies, and Paresh encouraged it. He shaped them."

"What frightens me is, how Paresh could come up with such a rigid idea, like the Caste!"

Meridian chimed in and said, "He didn't. According to what we know, Paresh learned about the Caste System from a relative of his. The idea was conceived by the featherless creatures we call Caretakers and Visitors. Their version is hereditary, and a birth determines a social status. Ours is designated by the color of our feathers. Evidently, their version is stricter."

"It's not exactly lenient here, if you'd consider the turkeys." Said Drazzle, frowning.

"I've an important question all my own," Zeet said.

"What is it, Zeet?" Delta asked.

Without hesitation, Zeet hopped in closer to Delta. "How come there aren't any cardinals in the Caste of Feathers?"

Chapter 37

Within the Posh Palace, Captain Pell had called for an emergency meeting.

The leader of the Phalanx of Pelicans stood before Paresh, who sat at the top of a stack of hay bales. It was his version of a throne. And next to his was another stack of hay, however, it wasn't as tall, which belonged to Paresh's wife, Prisha.

The room was well lit. Its walls were comprised of a minty green color. There were some food and water bowls placed neatly in a row. Also, inside this room was a small pool, shaped liked a turtle, colored in a bright green, which was used for the water fowl deemed privileged enough to enter the building.

In addition, there were items utilized by the Caretakers themselves, such as brooms, mops, and buckets, resting against the wall, to which they employed to maintain the Palace's tidiness.

The pheasant known as Cyril was also present, standing next to Pell. Due to the Captain's insistence, Paresh commanded everyone else to depart from the room.

"We've got a problem," said Captain Pell, without beating around the proverbial bush. "I've taken steps to stop it, but if it's not nipped in the bud, it's going to get worse."

From his vantage point, Paresh said, "Is Drazzle the detrimental cause to the discernable distress in your voice, Captain Pell?"

Pell said, with genuine amazement, "So, then, you are aware of the chatter circulating in the Caste."

Paresh suppressed a yawn. "Naturally."

"You must also know that Drazzle is under surveillance. I've ordered all my pelicans to keep a watchful eye on him. And it's a good thing I did. There was an incident recently involving the Untouchables. Drazzle was seen breaking the law and helping one of them with their chores."

Prisha was watching her husband closely. She was looking for a reaction to Pell's news. All she was really seeing was indifference. Or, was it an obscure arrogance? She looked at Cyril. He, like her, was silently listening.

Nonchalantly, Paresh said, "I trust, then, that Drazzle was reprimanded for his erroneous idealism? Was it impressed upon him the error of his ways in assisting non-entities?"

"In a way, yes," answered Pell. "Butterscotch told Drazzle it was against the law. But Drazzle explained to her why he was helping the old turkey, and it affected her. I think she was beginning to see it Drazzle's way. And you know how that hen loves to chinwag. I told her stop her clucking...or else. But I was too late, 'cause what happened with the Untouchables was made known to the other Caste members. Again, the Phalanx are trying to contain this, we're throwing our weight around, but I'm still sensing a...undercurrent, an echo, a residue. It's why, Potentate, I called for this meeting. You tasked me to protect the Caste, so let me do my duty."

Paresh appeared to look more interested, Prisha noticed. "And how, pray tell, do you intend to achieve that?" the Potentate wondered.

Pell's posture changed. He felt as if he was finally being taken seriously. "According to the latest surveillance report, Drazzle was seen leaving the habitat, with Zeet, Delta, and Meridian. This is an opportunity we can exploit to our benefit. Let me gather the combined might of the

Phalanx and block their reentrance. It's pretty obvious Delta and Meridian are lost causes. They're working with that loser of a duck. Let's exile them all from the Caste, for good."

Paresh looked away from Pell and set his eyes on Cyril. "As my Chief Aide, what is your reaction to these allegations, Cyril?"

Cyril said, as he bowed, "Indeed, I have heard correspondingly reverberations among adherents of the Caste. Still, at the present, it's merely gossip. I hardly think that's a concern for would-be insurrections. As for Mr. Fairfeather and his...incriminations...they're indicative of a novice, and..."

Pell interrupted Cyril, who was unmistakably offended by the pelican's outburst. "Again, with this excuse? He's *new*? If it were anyone else, they'd be gone. But I know what's really going on. It's the cardinal, isn't it? That little, loudmouth fleck of a bird!"

Paresh simply, yet inflexibly, answered, "Of course."

Pell was becoming angrier. "I've made it clear at the outset: I think Drazzle and Zeet are troublemakers. Indulging them, as you are, is dangerous. Keeping them here is gonna cost you."

Prisha immediately spoke, before Paresh could. She had a similar accent to her significant other, but her voice was more cloying. "Dear husband, Captain Pell is not prone to hyperbole. Perhaps you should heed his recommendation, and..."

Melodramatically, Paresh stood. "If you think...if anyone of you dare to think...I should fear some waddler from the wilderness, you have unacceptably underestimated me. I am this Caste's magnificent Potentate, thus I shall personally attend to this matter.

Once I am finished, your concerns will diminish, Captain. And a controlled decorum will resume itself."

Paresh paused for a moment, letting his edict sink in. He then spoke again, "Cyril, upon Drazzle's return to the habitat, tell him I wish to see him outside the Posh Palace, where we first met. Make it as clear as starlight that he is expected to come alone."

Chapter 38

Meridian was beside himself.

The mallard said, in an entreating voice, "Delta, this has already gone too far. If you tell Zeet what he wants to know, we've really broken the law. Let's just all go back to the habitat and try to live as normally as possible."

Delta raised her wing, a placating motion of halting her brother's protest. "We're standing on neutral ground, Meridian. There's no one around to inform on us. Besides, as I previously mentioned, we've already crossed a line. I have a notion there's no turning back, now."

Zeet looked more intrigued than before. Clearly, there was a story here.

Drazzle recognized it, too, but he stepped forward and said, "Delta, are you sure about this?"

Zeet, as well moved closer. "I hope she is, Drazzle. As a cardinal, I think I deserve to know what happened. It's pretty plain something did."

Delta nodded. "Let's continue to stroll, as we discuss the matter." She signaled with her neck and indicated which direction they should take. Zeet scurried through the grass, next to her, like a miniature red tumbleweed. Drazzle also followed, and Meridian was heard to say something rudely unintelligible under his breath, an expletive, and no one felt compelled to acknowledge him.

She steered them to what was called a gazebo. This small structure was colored in tan, and it had a dark blue triangular top and white lights spiraled around its eight columns.

"Our mother always liked this gazebo." Said Delta. Zeet flew and landed on the gazebo's railing, an ideal standpoint to listen to Delta. "Well, Zeet, there were actually cardinals in the Caste of Feathers. Two of them, in fact, a married couple. Their names were Redstrom and Veerness. When Cyril brought them to Paresh, he flattered them, and, as you were, Zeet, the Potentate assessed them and assigned Tiers. Redstrom, being bright red, was placed higher than his wife, since her feathers were mostly brown, despite having dashes of red in her beak, wings, and tail. Neither was thrilled about this separation, but in fairness to being new to the Caste, plus Paresh's wiles, they decided to cooperate."

"They were sporting folks," said Zeet, with pride. "So, what happened next, Delta?"

Meridian said, "Don't go on, Delta. It's dangerous. If the pelicans find out...!"

"Those bozos aren't here. What are you so afraid of?" Zeet chirped.

"Exile. And, Delta, I know you fear it, too."

Delta shuddered, Drazzle saw. Nevertheless, she overrode her trepidation and continued. "For Redstrom and Veerness, the breaking point arrived at lunch. The cardinals had different social statuses, so they couldn't eat together. Stormily, they protested about it. Paresh did his best to assuage them, yet to no avail. Paresh was forced to exile them. Which, of course, didn't really punish the couple, since they wanted out, anyway. Regardless, the Potentate declared it illegal to ever talk about that unceremonious moment. Personally, I always thought Paresh reacted the way he did because he was so humiliated and it was the first time he didn't get his way."

Zeet, overflowing with more cardinal pride, said, "Good for them! They felt exactly the way I did about

Paresh's stupid rules! I must've given the pompous peacock a bad case of familiarity!"

Meridian was pacing, visibly stressed. Drazzle had fallen silent. Meridian's aggravation was obvious, so Delta chose to address Drazzle, instead. "You're beginning to see, aren't you, Drazzle?"

"You bet, Delta. And you must, as well, Zeet. Remember when you made that comment about how Cyril looked at you, as if you were a juicy strawberry? Well, now, thanks to Delta being so forthcoming, we know Paresh wanted a replacement for his loss. It's the reason why Paresh tolerates me and makes concessions...it's all about you, Zeet."

Delta approached Drazzle and chummily placed her wing on his shoulder. "I'm sorry, my friend, but you are correct. That's the kind of hopeless bird ruling over us."

Meridian said, "Don't sell yourself short, Drazzle. As you already know, there aren't any white ducks in the Caste, so you do have some value to Paresh. And don't forget your flecks of yellow."

Although, it was an effort to be nice, Drazzle found no consolation in Meridian's words. There was a more pressing and nagging thought in his mind. "How long do I have, then?"

"I'm sorry?" came from Meridian.

"How long until I'm exiled? If Captain Pell is so worried about me, how much longer will Paresh tolerate me?"

"Paresh has a collector's mindset, Drazzle, and it's powerful. He wants to keep Zeet, and he knows you're a packaged deal, so he'll endure you for as long as possible."

"Delta's right," said Meridian. "But make no mistake, you've stirred things up in the Caste. The Phalanx tried to shut it down the gossip, but there's a residual resonance. As such, at best, you're probably on borrowed time."

Delta glared at her brother. "Aside from befriending me, maybe this is what the Wanderlust wanted for you, Drazzle, to introduce inspiration and change."

"*Aww*, come on, Delta! He's no messiah! He's a teenager, like us; and, as for being a symbol of social amendments, he's as *green* as my head!"

Delta whirled on Meridian. "I'm not asking him to be one! One thing is certain: he made the others think, and if they're thinking, maybe they'll realize this Caste system is repressive and they'll want to overturn it!"

"What happened to my meek sister? You're spewing treacherous words! You're risking our lives!"

Zeet said, in a sagely, country accent: "'The Wanderlust has something important for you to do, Drazzle, and there's no such thing as coincidence. It's gusting inside for you for a purpose. Let it guide you, my boy. You've got a great mind, and a caring heart. You'll prosper, and I just know it!'"

They all stared at the cardinal. Drazzle broke the silence. "He just quoted verbatim Q'teel, my Colony's Chief Founder. He said that at my grand farewell party."

Delta was moved, while Meridian was skeptical.

Drazzle said, "I've a suggestion, Delta and Meridian. What if Caste is incapable of change, and the Wanderlust brought me to rescue you both from it? We could leave here, together, right now, and embrace the outside world."

Delta's trepidation again seized her. "L-leave? We couldn't possibly do that! Without the Caretakers, who would look after us?

"It's totally possible to survive without them. Take my people, for example, they did it. I'm living proof of that accomplishment. I know the outside world seems really scary, I completely get it, but it's not all bad."

Meridian said, flatly, "Forget it, Drazzle."

Delta, more mildly, said, "We were hatched and raised here. This is our home, and it's still worth saving." She reached out to Drazzle, and, in turn, he reached out to her. "You reminded me of that, Drazzle. You reminded me what's important."

"Speaking of home," Meridian said, in a matter of fact sort of tone of voice, "We'd best get back to ours. The longer we're away, the more suspicious the Phalanx could become. We all understand each other better now, so that's got to count for something."

"It does." Said Drazzle and Delta, in unison.

Meridian grumbled a word in Mallardarian, and then took flight. Drazzle and Delta followed his example.

Still on the grassy ground, Zeet said to himself, "Mez and Vose, if only you could see your son, now. You, too, Q'teel. You'd be so proud. I know I am."

Happily, the cardinal ascended and pursued his companions.

Chapter 39

Upon their return, Cyril awaited them.

Meridian landed first and he immediately blanched. Or, at best, his green cheeks became a lighter tint.

"Chief Aide, what an unexpected pleasure!" Meridian said. It was a feigned, pleased reaction, but the mallard hoped it was enough to convince the pheasant.

Cyril bypassed the pleasantry, whether it was real, or otherwise, and solely addressed Drazzle, as the white duck made his landing.

"Mister Fairfeather, I was sent to inform you that the Potentate wishes an audience with you, outside the Posh Palace, at once."

Delta waddled next to Drazzle. "May I come, too, sir?" said Delta.

Cyril slowly shook his head. "I fear not, Miss Webbingston. This summons is an exclusive one."

Zeet returned to the ground, and said, "What's going on?"

Drazzle answered, "The Potentate wants to see me, Zeet."

Zeet scuttled to Drazzle's side. "Well, let's go, then."

Delta put out a wing and waved back his friend. "Not this time, Zeet. It's a private meeting."

Cyril superciliously sniffled, and said, "Indeed. And time is of the essence. It is impolite to tarry."

"I'll be back soon, I'm sure." Drazzle said. He smiled at his friends, but it was a forced countenance. In truth, he was very nervous. Notwithstanding this fact, he took flight, a faster means to reach his destination.

Cyril offered a short bow to the remaining trio, and then took his leave.

"This was exactly what I feared." Said Meridian, as soon as Cyril was far enough away. "Drazzle's borrowed time? It might be up."

"Don't say such things, Meridian." Said Delta, boldly.

"Whatever happens next, we must support our friend. Because that's exactly what he'd do for us."

Chapter 40

As when they were first introduced, Paresh was sitting on his grey ledge.

Drazzle landed beneath him. Drazzle looked around and saw no pelicans. Apparently, this really was a private meeting.

From his perch, Paresh said, "Thank you for coming so swiftly. I appreciate punctuality in my subjects. You'll understand, I trust, why we cannot have our discussion inside the Posh Palace, because you are unworthy to enter it."

Paresh leaped to Drazzle. "Let me begin by saying, it must be truly difficult being new, especially with your *humble* and *rustic* background."

Drazzle sensed Paresh was trying to be congenial, but the connotation seemed more disingenuous.

Standing face to face, the peacock said, "But cheer up! I am present to offer you guidance! I have decided to personally take you under my wing and teach you some life lessons. Why, before long, I predict you'll take to things very well, much like a duck does to water!"

It was a jape thinly disguised as encouragement. It was one of his talents, using upbeat words fluidly to act approachable and patronizing simultaneously. And he presented himself so confidently. When Drazzle was first assessed, he was extremely nervous, but this encounter exceeded that. As before, all he could muster at the moment was to listen.

"I want you to tell me something—and please be truthful—because this is incredibly important. What was the first thing you noticed about our darling Delta Webbingston?"

Drazzle opened himself to his mind's-eye and recalled the memory. It was really none of the Potentate's business, but Drazzle answered regardless. "I...I thought she was beautiful. I...I had never beheld a duck as she before. It may sound silly, but I remember thinking a tree and the sky donated their colors to her. She looked so lovely, sitting there, as she was, with those alliums behind her. She was a vision."

The peacock smiled, a genuine one, even, and was decidedly pleased with Drazzle's rhetoric. "Yes, I imagine her visage made quite an impact, given you hail from a mostly monochromatic culture, I suspect. No, Drazzle, it doesn't sound silly at all. In fact, you saw the only thing that really mattered about her."

Drazzle couldn't conceal his confusion. "Sir?"

"Walk with me, and I shall enlighten you." Said Paresh. Drazzle nervously joined him, as they walked together along the perimeter of the Posh Palace.

"You see, Drazzle, fundamentally, in all existence, our appearances, our exteriors, they hold true significance. Indeed, we're continuously judged by them. After all, the Visitors judged me, and recognized my handsomeness. It's because of them I became the Potentate. Thus, these decrees determine our worth in life. It's the reason why first impressions are so important.

Drazzle paused in his waddling. "With respect, sir, that's just the surface stuff. Since you mentioned Delta specifically, what about her personality? What about her brilliant mind? What of the content of her very soul?"

Paresh also stopped walking and vainly gazed at his talons. "*Oh*. Yes. *Those things*. I won't fully dismiss them, since character does play a role in judgments. My disposition, of course, is scintillating. However, temperament is still secondary. Again, I cannot stress this enough, it's the outer package that holds all the true value."

Drazzle continued to look confounded. Paresh observed this, and resumed strolling. Drazzle followed. Soon enough, they were side by side, once more.

"Let's approach this another way, shall we? Tell me, have you ever stopped to ponder Zeet's resplendent red feathers?"

Drazzle shrugged. "No, not really. He's my friend. That's what surely counts with me."

Paresh said, "How touching, how quaint", while he rolled his eyes. "Anyway, there are three facets to birdkind that contribute to our diversity. For instance, there is pigmentation, which are shown in us and other creatures, as well as plant life. Pertaining to us, Drazzle, we birds are granted our myriad colorization as a result of three elements, which are known as carotenoids, melanins, and porphyrines."

Drazzle had never heard this before. Admittedly, he was intrigued.

"Fashioned by flora, carotenoids are responsible for Zeet's cerise. For this to occur, he had to consume a plant, or he ate something that had already eaten one. Interestingly, carotenoids interconnect with melanins, and they initiate fascinating colors!"

As he spoke, Paresh was becoming more passionate. Obviously, this was a lecture he treasured and enjoyed imparting to a recipient. And, of course, Drazzle knew why Paresh was spending the effort on him. Primarily, it was about Zeet. If Paresh wanted to keep Zeet in the Caste, he needed to convince Drazzle that his social system was effective, ergo ending his disruptive presence as a 'nuisance.'

Drazzle couldn't point out the specialized knowledge about Redstrom and Veerness, because it would implicate Delta and Meridian, and they've both already risked plenty in order to be straightforward about the origin of the Caste.

"And what are melanins? I am glad you asked, Drazzle!"

Of course, Drazzle didn't ask, but he remained silent and let the peacock flute on.

"As diminutive granules of hues, in the feathers and the skin, melanins manifest in our kind. Aggregation and section, these factors make melanins contingent, and they can yield an assortment of colors. Incidentally, melanins afford more than the colorization, of course. Indeed, when feathers comprise melanin, they are consequently robust and resilient, as opposed to those without."

Paresh snatched a grasshopper from the ground and ate it. "And, finally," he said. "Let me discuss porphyrins. Indeed, it's another pigment set, created by varying amino acids. In case you aren't familiar with amino acids, they're essentially organic compounds that encompass together amino and carboxylic acid, purposeful collections. At any rate, porphyrins may diverge in chemical configuration. Notwithstanding this, they interestingly have something in common: when subjected to ultraviolet light, they incandesce in bright red; similarly in a manner particular rocks and minerals have a reputation for doing the same. Fascinatingly, porphyrins induce an array of hues, such as browns, reds, greens, and pink."

So enthralled was Drazzle, he didn't immediately realize the peacock had conveniently led him to the

Pyramid of Configuration. No, Drazzle thought, this was contrived, just like everything Paresh does.

With a grandiose gesture, Paresh directed Drazzle to the schematic of the Caste. "When you take all that I have taught you in account, it requires someone with a discriminating eye to sort out this gallimaufry of colors, to make sense of it all. That's my purpose, Drazzle. I created order by making a perfect social system for everyone."

Drazzle studied Paresh, who was intoxicated with his self-importance. It was troubling.

Drazzle said, "But, sir, how can any social system be considered perfect when you have some of its members feel like nothing. I know this for a fact, because one of the turkeys..."

Paresh cut him off. "An Untouchable, you mean? That's their designation, Drazzle."

"My apologies, but that word sounds awful."

Indifferently Paresh said, "That's their designation."

Drazzle pointed to the bottom of the Caste Pyramid. "Their elder told me himself that they're nothing, and they weren't worth helping. To me, that's wrong. I still feel ashamed I stopped helping that senior bird. He shouldn't have been forced to work like that, given his age."

"May I remind you, Drazzle, it is illegal to assist the Untouchables? You're fortunate I didn't have you penalized for that mistake."

Again, Drazzle thought to himself, this 'mercy' was because of Zeet, but he held his tongue.

"Moreover," continued the Potentate. "It was I who decided that they're Untouchables. Thus, it was decree to sentence them to the bottom of the Pyramid and assign to them their labors."

"But why does it have to be them??"

"They're hideous, that's why! Have you honestly looked at them? Nature dealt them a bad destiny, plain and simple! Consequently, someone has to attend to the commonplace duties of the Caste! The grotesque must serve their betters!"

Drazzle was getting mad. "I'm aware you're knowledgeable, and, yes, you're attractive, but are those really good reasons to oversee a society?"

Paresh was likewise fuming. "You apparently haven't accurately beheld me, in my natty feathers! In all superb majesty!

Abruptly, quickly, his train of feathers developed into his showy fan of feathers. Only this time, the fan fervently vibrated, like a squall through switchgrass. All those 'eyes' were eerily stationary, while feathers rattled. Being this close to the spectacle was terrifying, and Drazzle immobilized. Drazzle found himself immersed in the rippling shadow of Paresh's exhibition.

Suddenly, the shaking stopped, and Paresh spoke, "Now, stripling, that I have your full attention, I must say, if you insist on being impertinent, if you refuse to take me seriously, I will respond more forcefully. I am demanding your obedience. If you won't acquiesce, I shall banish Delta."

Drazzle, still scared, managed to say, "That's kind of an empty threat. There's a farm here. She could go there." Even Drazzle was shocked those words had fallen from his bill, but desperate times and all!

Paresh laughed, unkindly. "Perhaps at one point, yet no longer. Yes, a duck could visit the farm, but it's only temporary. Nowadays, the Caretakers return any bird, not a chicken or a rooster, back to this habitat. So, Drazzle, that option is not viable."

"Why should I believe you?"

"As your Potentate, I've no cause to lie to you. As such, I should inform you there's another meaning to the word 'exile.' When I said, I would banish Delta, I didn't mean just from this habitat, and not simply from the zoo itself...I meant it in a very final sense of the definition."

"Y-you couldn't possibly..."

"Go ahead and test my conviction." said Paresh, coldly.

They shared locked stares. It was a showdown of wills. Who would first buckle?

It was Drazzle. Defeated, he said, "What must I do to keep her safe from you?"

"It's quite simple, Drazzle. Inform the others that you support my Caste. Tell them I am a wonderful leader. Recant your previous observations and admit that you were wrong."

Drazzle lowered his head. His eyes glistened with tears. "I'll do it."

"Splendid. Now, off with you, now, and do my bidding."

Drazzle turned away. Then, he paused. Looking back at Paresh, Drazzle said, "Paresh..." Under the circumstances, he ignored his manners and chose to address the peacock informally, "I've seen your true colors, and I've no problem in saying to you, they're repugnant."

Undaunted, Paresh countered, "Spoken like a real philistine. Only this one is going to repent. Welcome back to the fold, Drazzle."

Chapter 39

When Drazzle returned to his three friends, he saw that they weren't alone.

All the turkeys of the Caste were present, which all their eyes were trained on the white duck.

Again, no pelicans were in view, however, Meridian seemed anxious. He looked left, then right, as if he was expecting to see the Phalanx, too.

Zeet appeared to be happy to see his friend.

Delta was smiling, a pacifying one. She said, "Welcome back, Drazzle. Is everything all right?"

Drazzle replied, yet not in the way she had asked. He was addressing the presence of the turkeys.

"What's all this?" asked Drazzle.

Delta said, "The turkeys have something to say to you, Drazzle."

One of the turkeys stepped forward. He looked to be another teenager, young and vital. He said, "My name is Trevor. First, we want to thank you for showing our elder dignity. In doing so, you did this for all of us. Honestly, we're not used to being treated with respect. Second, if you have come to bring change to the Caste, we want you to know, we're behind you. Whatever you need, we'll stand by you, Drazzle."

Drazzle had opened his mouth to respond, but before he could form the words, the aforementioned elder emerged from the back of the cadre of turkeys.

"Young one," said the elder, to Drazzle, in a deep, tired voice. "Don't feel pressured to accept. The risk of exile is too great. We're Untouchables, and we're not worthy of such philanthropy."

"No!" snapped Trevor. "With respect, Theodore, we deserve better! Drazzle would make a better leader than Paresh! It's time for a change!"

Drazzle was looking overwhelmed. Delta, sensing this, reached out and rested her wing on his shoulder.

"I agree with Trevor. I'm not ashamed to admit it, change is scary. But so is complacency, especially an unfair and outdated version of it. What I'm trying to say is, I'm on your side, too."

Complacency. There, again, was the term. Q'teel had used the word, and said it blinded the Colony from recognizing the Wanderlust in Drazzle. In the Caste, it was empowering a rigid social structure.

"You know you can count on me, Drazzle!" cheered Zeet. "Through thick or thin, best friend, always!"

With his wingtip, Meridian rubbed his forehead, as if trying to rid himself of a headache. Decidedly, he was still divided about this development. Meridian soon realized everyone was staring at him. Wordlessly, he nodded his consent.

Unexpectedly, Drazzle wrenched himself away from Delta, which subsequently startled her. Both Meridian and Zeet were also nonplussed. Even the turkeys were confounded. Delta asked, "Drazzle, what's wrong??"

Drazzle didn't hesitate to answer. "Look, I'm flattered by all the faith you have in me. But it's totally misplaced. I mean, what do I *know* about how a society should be maintained? I'm still practically a boy! I—I was wrong to question Paresh and his Caste. So very wrong!"

The abrupt silence was thunderous. Everyone was stationary, stupefied. Howsoever, all save for one. Zeet hopped forward. "Something happened with Paresh, didn't it? What was said between you two?"

Drazzle looked away. Zeet persevered. "Paresh said something to sway you, didn't he? It's the only explanation for this hasty change of opinion. Paresh said something terrible, I'll bet. I'm right, aren't I?"

Drazzle still didn't reply. He kept his eyes trained on the ground. Zeet said, "Did....did Paresh make a threat?"

More silence from Drazzle. Zeet drew closer to his best friend. "You're protecting one of us, aren't you? I don't think it's me, because Paresh has waited too long for a cardinal to be added to the Caste. And, no offense, Meridian, I doubt this has anything to do with you. On second thought, it really does. Paresh threatened Delta, right, Drazzle?"

Drazzle began to cry. He couldn't restrain it. In an anguished whisper, Drazzle said, "Yes!"

Delta shuddered. Meridian was beyond himself and shouted, "That monster! How dare he threaten my sister! Drazzle, what exactly did he say??"

"Please, Meridian, I can't talk about it. I-I've already said too much. If you care about Delta, as much as I do, you'll just stop. Conform to the Caste, like I have, and she'll be safe."

"I really must know, Drazzle. What will Paresh do to her?"

"H-he'll exile her, Meridian. Just not in the sense you fear. It's much worse. He'll banish Delta, in a final way. I...I can't bear the thought of it. I agreed to stop making trouble for Paresh. I must! He's so in love with power, he'll do anything to keep it!"

Delta came forward. "That reason alone is why this cannot continue. We must stop this. It's gone too far."

Meridian said, "I agree. I know I dithered before, but I see that pretentious exhibitionist for what he really is!"

Trevor joined the conversation. "We're with you, as well."

The senior turkey was quiet. His head was lowered, and his eyes were set on the floor.

Drazzle tried to placate the stressful situation. "No! You can't go against Paresh! We've got to protect Delta!"

"I couldn't agree more."

Everyone pivoted. There was Prisha, the First Lady, Paresh's peafowl wife. Standing behind her was the entire Phalanx of Pelicans, in a perfect row, with Captain Pell, at the center.

"Fortunately, I've a perfect solution," said Prisha, in her saccharine tone of voice. "You, Drazzle, and Zeet, and Delta, and Meridian, will all be leaving here tonight. The Phalanx will escort you, to ensure your departure."

Chapter 40

It became so quiet, you could have heard an acorn drop.

Everyone was stunned by this sudden arrival of visitors. Since joining the Caste, Drazzle hadn't any contact with Prisha. Drazzle only saw her when she and Paresh made their grand dancing entrance, and at various mealtimes.

Captain Pell was looking cocky, just like always. The other pelicans stood at attention.

Prisha said, finally, ""The Phalanx of Pelicans will usher you to the fence. Once there, you'll all depart. And, I don't simply mean from the habitat, but the entire zoo. I expect you to never return. Should you refuse to leave, the Phalanx are encouraged to utilize force."

If Prisha's voice had a fragrance, it would be a gardenia. She spoke of potential violence, yet her syrupy tone made it sound so casual and innocent.

"Ma'am?" said Drazzle, clearly confused.

"You sound muddled. Was I not concise enough for you?"

"I...I made a deal with your husband, ma'am. Has the Potentate changed his mind? Did he send you to tell me differently?"

Prisha smiled, prettily. "I'm perfectly aware he was going to exchange words with you and attempt to persuade you to our cause. No, my dear, Paresh hasn't had any second thoughts. Your arrangement stills stands. However, I'm here to offer you another, which would be less harsh, yet unconditional."

Obviously, Prisha had eavesdropped on their conversation, Drazzle thought to himself. She and the Phalanx had approached, without their knowledge, because they were all distracted. What Drazzle failed to understand was, why was Prisha going behind her husband's back?

Ironically, it was as if Prisha was privy to Drazzle's thoughts, because she answered his question. As she talked, she moved among Drazzle and his friends. She outright refused to look at the turkeys. She acted like they weren't even there.

"You see, Drazzle, I happen to love my lifestyle. Paresh and I, we have striven to meticulously shape a flawless society. I'm completely besotted with having power and influence. Therefore, I will do what is necessary to safeguard our top positions in the Caste. Paresh thinks he's doing what's right, since he's fixated on the cardinal. Since he lost the others, he's always yearned to have another. But that obsession is dangerous. Captain Pell knows it, too. He tried to warn Paresh, but my husband wasn't truly listening. I was, though. That's why I'm taking control of this matter."

Prisha turned and looked directly at Delta. "Suppose Paresh did order Captain Pell to 'banish' Delta, you could become an even greater problem. Martyrdom is something never to underestimate, especially since such an outcome has never been explored before, and the Caretakers would not approve."

Again, because of her honeyed inflection, Prisha made the idea of harming someone so nonchalant.

But, aside from that, Drazzle heard something else. Something, in fact, which could be useful, if handled adroitly.

Prisha finally regarded the turkeys. The way she went about it, however, was with abhorrence, as if the very acknowledgment of them was excruciating.

"As for you, Untouchables, I suspect you are wondering why I haven't ordered your dismissal. Before the Phalanx exiles these four, I actually wanted you to witness how your superiors can rectify a most distasteful situation. Whatever hope you were embracing, I am ending it, right now. Captain Pell, I do believe they've seen enough. I tire of their sight. Send them away."

Captain Pell came forward and snarled, "All right, you pathetic losers, it's time for you to go back to your lousy corner of the habitat."

The turkeys, except for the elder, formed their own line, directly before Drazzle.

"Are you as deaf as you are ugly? I said, go back!" Pell barked.

The turkeys were resolute, and they wouldn't budge. Trevor said, "Before the Caste was founded, turkeys were treated fairly and decently. The other birds, they went along with it. But Drazzle shook things up. And you're really worried about that, otherwise you wouldn't be going to such trouble to be rid of him and the others. Drazzle's our hero, our inspiration, and we're not going to back down!"

"I'm standing with them, too!" Meridian announced, proudly.

Delta left Drazzle's side, and joined her brother. "It was intimidation which led Drazzle to negotiate for my wellbeing. That's Paresh's stock-in-trade. But it was my fear that really made it possible. It's time for me to take responsibility for my welfare and cast off the fear."

The elder turkey floundered to the others. "I was convinced that my fellow turkeys and I were nonentities. Our peers made us feel this way, as Trevor indicated. It was wrong of us to succumb. It was especially wrong for everyone else to comply with our degradation. No more, I say."

Drazzle was honored. He could hardly believe his presence was so influential. Yet, there they were, these courageous birds, rallying against oppression. But he saw a possible solution to end this. He just needed to get everyone's attention. Before he could shape the words, Captain Pell bellowed, "Phalanx--attack!!"

Chapter 41

Butterscotch always went on a saunter, in the morning.

It was important for her to preserve her health. After all, by her definition, she was no longer a spring chicken. As she bobbed along the grass, pecking her insects, she heard strident voices.

She conceded to her curiosity and proceeded in the direction of those voices. There was the potential to learn of some juicy gossip to share. After all, unofficially, she felt it was her duty to keep everyone informed.

When she arrived, she saw the First Lady, and the Phalanx, on one side, and Drazzle, and his friends, on the other. Most curious of all, was the presence of the turkeys. Given what she had recently witnessed with Drazzle and the Untouchables, Butterscotch assumed this encounter must share a connection.

The tension in the air was palpable. Insofar as, no one was cognizant Butterscotch was watching. Surreptitiously, she positioned herself behind a bush, and listened to the exchanges. She peaked through openings in the greenery.

Butterscotch was astounded by everything she heard. She was seized with dread when Captain Pell commanded his fellow pelicans to attack!

She saw the pelicans rush forward, with their large wings flapping madly, and their huge pouch-mouths gaping.

In turn, the turkeys responded, as they dashed to action. They would jump and thrust their chests against the pelicans. In turn, the pelicans attempted to bite them.

Captain Pell targeted Drazzle, but Zeet intervened. Furiously, the cardinal pecked at Pell's head. Agitatedly, Pell shook his head, trying to avoid the little bird's assault.

"Get away from me, you pesky twerp!" hissed Pell.

"You were going to hurt my best friend! That's something I'll never allow!" Zeet remarked.

Drazzle screamed, "Zeet, be careful! He could swallow you up!"

"It'd be worth it, to keep you safe! You guys should get Delta to safety, fast! I've got this!"

"Zeet's got the right idea, Drazzle!" Meridian said, as he started to nudge Drazzle and Delta both in the direction of a nearby tree.

"Getting gulped by a raging pelican is the right idea??"

"Of course not! You know what I meant!" If Paresh ordered them to hurt Delta, we've got to get her away from this fighting!"

The three ducks took refuge behind the tree. Meridian took a peak around its corner. "They're still going at it, turkeys and pelicans alike," said Meridian. "Zeet's okay, and still engaging Pell."

"Thank goodness!" sighed Drazzle. "What's Prisha doing?"

Meridian shook his head. "She's doing nothing, that's what. Now, I could be mistaken, but she looks overwhelmed. She's standing on the sidelines of the brawling. Prisha could end of this, yet she doesn't seem inclined."

Delta whispered to herself, "This is horrible. In the history of the habitat, we've never warred against one another. It's so awful, shameful. I was hoping words would bring about change, not violence." She turned to Drazzle. "How can we stop this madness??"

Drazzle said, "Delta, I think I know a way out of this. First, though, I've a very important question to ask you."

Butterscotch felt conflicted. Shouldn't she report this to someone in authority, such as the Chief Aide? Or, the Potentate himself? However, she was afraid to get involved. Sternly, Captain Pell warned her not to talk about what happened with Drazzle and the Untouchables. He threatened her with exile. Ergo, she stopped talking about it. However, Drazzle's nobility still haunted her, and it was her own ignominy that compelled Butterscotch to even broach the topic with the other birds. She felt trapped between her self-preservation, and her conscience.

As fast as her legs would carry her, she ran for help.

Chapter 42

The Captain of Phalanx was becoming vexed.

He was thinking this confrontation was taking too long. The Untouchables were encouraged by a false notion of hope, instigated by Drazzle and his friends. It made them fight on uncompromisingly.

And this twerp of a cardinal was equally persistent with his pecking barrage. Captain Pell feigned pain, as if Zeet had pecked one of his eyes. Zeet hesitated, aloft, concerned he went too far. As he would a gnat, Pell used his wing and swatted Zeet away. The small red bird tumbled through the air, and crashed to the ground, a few paces away from the Captain.

From their hiding spot, Meridian announced, "*Oh*, no! Pell just clobbered Zeet!"

"NO!" yelled Drazzle, as he dashed away from the tree. Delta followed, and so did Meridian. Drazzle went to Zeet's side and asked, "My friend, tell me you're all right, please!"

Zeet said, raspy, "Y-yeah...I'll be...fine. Big...galoot...got the...best of me. I'll...be...fine...once these...hummingbirds...stop spinning...'round my head."

Drazzle turned to Zeet's assailant and said, "You're a monster, Pell!"

"Maybe, but I'm a victorious one." Pell ran to Torrance, whom, until now, was ignored by both warring parties. "Now, listen up, everyone! Either you surrender to us, right now, or this geezer gets it!" Perilously, the pelican opened his mouth wide around the elder turkey's trembling head. Given the strength of Pell's jaw, he could seriously harm Torrance.

All the turkeys froze. Consternation was written on their faces.

Prisha recovered her bravery and stood next to Pell. In her flowery manner of voice, she said, "I'd heed Captain Pell, if I were you. Thankfully, I'm blessed, so I'm glad I'm not anything like you, though." She giggled at her own witticism.

Drazzle told Delta, "Please, look after Zeet." Next, Drazzle waddled past the motionless turkeys and approached Prisha and Pell, the latter still maintaining his aggressive pose.

"I think it's time for you to really prioritize what's important to you, Captain. Is Paresh and Prisha...and their Caste system...really worth your freedom? Your life, for that matter? While you all were fighting, I asked Delta what would happen to a bird that would seriously hurt another...or do worse! It's something you already know, but you've gotten so absorbed in enforcing social order, it was easier for you to become bullies and uphold intimidations. And why not? I mean, you had the prestige of a higher Tier. Not to mention, you're bigger birds, and you have numbers on your side. Until now, you never really had to resort to brute force. Prisha proved it, a moment ago, when she said the Caretakers wouldn't approve."

Prisha's winced. She didn't savor the idea of her own words used against her.

Drazzle continued his monologue. "In a zoo, the Caretakers are responsible for you. They tend to your needs. They *know* you. They'll distinguish who inflicted certain wounds. Delta said when a denizen of the zoo does something like that, they're evaluated. They could be placed in isolation, while answers are explored. They may return to the habitat. Then again, you may get transferred to another zoo, and lose what you knew and had. Or, in more extreme circumstances, you could be euthanized. Delta taught me that word. Again, I'll ask you, Captain, is the Caste worth taking a life? Is it worth risking your own??"

Captain Pell's yellow eyes blazed with fury. Slowly, his bill and throat pouch began to shut. Then, he paused, and closed his eyes. When he reopened his eyes, that aforementioned fury was extinguished. Pell withdrew his menacing posture. Next, he said, "Phalanx, stand down.'

One of the bewildered pelicans asked, "Sir?"

More resolutely, Pell said, "Stand down, I said. It's...over."

Prisha could hardly believe it! "Captain, y-you cannot give up. Y-you mustn't!"

The First Lady soon realized an audience had manifested. It was comprised of Butterscotch, white geese, roosters, songbirds, Canada geese, mallards, and hens.

Butterscotch was standing in the front.

Prisha tried to regain control of her situation. With a contrived sense of composure, she said, "*Ah*, excellent. You've arrived just in time. Your First Lady needs you. In the name of our glorious Potentate, I command you to evict Drazzle and these other traitors. And, make no mistake, I am including the disappointing Phalanx."

Prisha's edict washed over them. They processed it all. They looked at Prisha, and they looked at Drazzle.

The Canada geese reacted with bent necks, and they hissed contemptibly at Prisha. "*Ahhhh!*" Prisha gasped out, visibly startled by their insubordination. Suddenly, she felt so outnumbered and alone.

Butterscotch said, "I was hidden behind that bush, over there, and I saw everything. It wasn't easy for me, because I was scared, but I knew I couldn't live with myself, if I had done nothing and looked the other way."

Butterscotch approached Drazzle. "You opened my eyes, sugar. You left an impression on me I couldn't shake off. When you helped Torrance...yes, I'm actually addressing him by name...I said you were degrading yourself. In truth, *I* was degrading myself, 'cause I had accepted it was perfectly fine to think of other folks as less, just 'cause they look different. I was wrong. We were wrong. That's why I rallied the others you see here, right now. They believed me when I told them what was going on. And we believe in you, Drazzle."

Meanwhile, within the Posh Palace, Paresh was holding court. Three of his favorite Caste members were present: Cyril, Florida, and Concerto. Atop his throne of bales of hay, Paresh was feeling particularly proud of himself. After all, he was successful in converting Drazzle to his cause. His charismatic authority was still intact. Best of all, Paresh could keep his cardinal. Subsequently, his Caste of Feathers felt even more whole.

Imagine, then, his astonishment when Drazzle strolled into view.

And Drazzle wasn't alone. Delta and Meridian were with him.

Cyril immediately incepted the newcomers before they got closer. "Mr. Webbingston, you, of course, are permitted to be here. However, *they* are not. You know the rules."

Meridian said, "Tell me, Cyril, when you ever saw me come in? I never did, since it didn't seem fair that my sister couldn't come inside, especially when the weather turned colder. If she had to brave the elements, I would do the same."

Cyril was unimpressed. "I am failing to comprehend the relevance of your statement."

Paresh stood up. "How did you get past my Phalanx guards?"

Drazzle said, "Yes, about that…" The white duck gestured in a certain direction. Captain Pell came into view. Behind him followed some pelicans, along with Prisha.

Prisha ran to her husband, who had leaped to the floor. "*Oh*, Paresh, it's horrendous! The Phalanx have turned against us!"

Paresh was becoming fraught. "That's impossible! Their function is to serve and protect the Caste!"

The Potentate scowled at Drazzle. "What have you done, Drazzle? I thought we had an arrangement!"

Cyril looked skeptically at Paresh. Florida and Concerto watched with a keen focus.

"We did, Paresh. I was totally prepared to honor it, too. I'd do anything to keep Delta safe. But, I must tell you, your wife didn't like our deal. She knew it wouldn't stand, so she made her own ultimatum. Prisha tried to force the three of us into exile. However, an unexpected development happened."

Again, Drazzle gestured, and in came the turkeys. Torrance was in the front of the group.

"The turkeys have had enough.

Paresh was now infuriated. "They're called 'Untouchables'! How dare they pollute the Posh Palace?! This defilement is intolerable! Get out! GET OUT!!"

Torrance said, in a trembling voice, "It's been so long since any of us had seen the inside of this sanctuary. I almost had forgotten how it looked."

Delta stood next to Torrance. "I know the feeling. It feels wonderful to be back."

Paresh: "Well, don't get comfortable! Captain Pell, just don't stand there! Do your duty! Evict them all!!"

None of the pelicans moved a muscle. In desperation, Paresh turned to Prisha. "Drazzle is lying! He must be! You would never go against me!"

Prisha said nothing. But Captain Pell said, "In all the time I served you, I never lied to you. It's over, Paresh. I won't risk my place in the habitat."

Paresh was disconcerted. "I...I don't understand. What does that mean?"

Drazzle replied, "It means, Paresh, that they value the Caretakers more, over you. And without the pelicans to enforce your Caste policies, there is no longer a Caste."

Paresh said, "B-but I am revered by the Visitors! I am the star attraction! There's not another bird more incandescent than I! To go against me, is to go against them! You worshipped me—I gave you a perfect society!"

Drazzle shook his head. "You used the Visitors and the Caretakers against the Community to make a perfect society for *yourself*. There just wasn't a fence surrounding this habitat, you designed a border of vanity to enclose the others. Complacency kept it going, but that's ending."

Paresh said, pleading, "W-what about those of you that I uplifted to a higher status? Cyril? Florida? Concerto?"

Cyril ignored Paresh and approached Torrance. "I am so ashamed of my role in this tawdry affair. Torrance...all of you...could you ever forgive me?"

Torrance said, "Of course, Cyril. But let us not dwell on the past. It is the future we should now consider and shape accordingly."

Florida said, "I can still be fabulous without a silly Tier. It's not worth having, anyway, if others are miserable."

Concerto surprised everyone most of all. For as a mute swan, this was the first time that she ever spoke. Her fancy accent matched her refinement. "I say, this indignity cannot continue. I renounce my role in the Caste, as so many have forsaken it."

Ardent applause ensured. Paresh whirled on Prisha. "This is your fault! You just had to interfere! I told you I would attend to the matter! I never should have shared power with someone as...as unadorned as you!"

Prisha was discernably hurt by her husband's cruel words, and she slapped him.

Drazzle said, "You both have a choice: either accept the ending of the Caste and renounce your rulership, or be forced into exile yourselves. And just let me say, given how pampered you two were, I don't foresee you lasting very long in the outside world."

Fear took Paresh and Prisha both. Simultaneously, they nodded their capitulation.

Epilogue

In the next few days, things moved quickly after Paresh and Prisha relinquished control.

To commemorate the auspicious beginning for the Fellowship of Feathers, the new title of their society, which all the birds in the habitat reached a consensus, the Pyramid of Configuration was dismantled. The substituting name 'Fellowship of Feathers' was an amalgamation of the past and the future. It signified revision and the result of mutual betterment.

The building once known as the Posh Palace was rechristened as the Haven for All.

Drazzle and Delta were nominated for leadership roles, but both declined. Instead, they proposed a democracy, where every bird dwelling in the habitat had a voice, and the colors of their feathers mattered not in the process.

Zeet had recovered nicely from his assault from Captain Pell. In fact, subsequently, he became famous among the songbirds, especially those of who weren't very receptive in the beginning to Zeet, when he had first arrived at the zoo. They were so impressed with how the cardinal took on a bird much larger than himself, they treated Zeet with more respect, and since the Caste policies were rendered immaterial, they welcomed him into their fellowship.

The turkeys were treated better with greater respect. No longer seen as lowly 'Untouchables', they could dine with everyone else. Interestingly, they continued to keep the habitat nice and tidy, but it was their decision to do so. It was no longer illegal to aid them, which many of the other birds shared in this responsibility. Torrance formed a fast friendship with Cyril, and the pair enjoyed discussing philosophy.

Captain Pell and the pelicans stayed united and were renamed as the Peacekeepers, since the Phalanx had a negative connotation. Of course, they recanted their bullying tactics, but, as a precaution, Meridian worked with them closely. The mallard served a role similar to Drazzle's father, Mez, the Director of Defense, back home.

The squirrels, who were denied access to their nuts under the old regime, were welcomed back and encouraged to reclaim what was theirs. In addition, as a gesture of reparation, the squirrels were asked to share the birds' food and water.

Paresh didn't adapt well at all to his new circumstances. He found it challenging, not being the center of attention. Paresh lost interest in performing for the Visitors, and, despite Drazzle's magnanimous attempts to include him in the Fellowship, he ironically sequestered himself to the lonely corner, where the turkeys were once forced to live. Paresh only made appearances for food and water.

Conversely, Prisha sought redemption. After realizing Paresh never really cared for her, Prisha dissolved their marriage. She discovered what was really important, and, instead of championing practices of vanity, Prisha acted as a counselor of a type, fostering a healthier self-image for all.

Butterscotch became an official narrator. Since she was so adroit at telling stories, she was appointed to disseminate how this new epoch got started. Indeed, a vital component of that change was the Wanderlust, which was celebrated by the Fellowship of Feathers. For it was this phenomenon that delivered a facilitator of change, an actual hero, in many birds' eyes.

The irony was not lost on Drazzle. The Wanderlust chose Q'teel to lead his people to a new place to settle, far away from the domineering Farmers. When the Wanderlust selected Drazzle, it delivered him to a home maintained by the same featherless creatures he was taught to fear, but the Caretakers were very different from the Farmers. Tream was ultimately correct. They weren't all the same.

Drazzle couldn't be gladder for his new home because he made actual friends...and more.

Zephyr gently bent the purple alliums, where Drazzle initially met Delta. Alone, at last, they shared their first kiss.

The future looked bright.

Acknowledgements

First and foremost, I'd like to thank my parents, Mary Ann and Ken Johnson, for giving me life. I wish to express immense gratitude to my Mother for always standing by my side. Together, we've been through thick and thin. Moreover, when I would yield to my procrastination, she would encourage me to write by giving me a deadline. I love you dearly, Mother.

I also want to warmly thank my best friend, Andrew Sheldon, for approaching me about publishing a book. This was a dream of mine and having gone through the publication process himself, his advice and guidance was truly invaluable.

In addition, many glorious thanks go to my beta readers, Patty Vance and Janet Keith. Both of whom were instrumental with their generous feedback. The former thoroughly edited my work and helped me clean up my punctuation problems and diction.

And finally, I wish to convey grand appreciation to you, my readers, for taking a chance and exploring my first book. If I've done my job correctly, then I hope you enjoyed Drazzle's story.

References

Bull, J. L., Farrand, J., & Bull, J. L. (2004). National Audubon Society Field Guide to North American birds. Knopf.

Thompson, M. (2015, August 11). How birds make colorful feathers: Bird academy • the Cornell lab. Bird Academy. https://academy.allaboutbirds.org/how-birds-make-colorful-feathers/

Google. (n.d.). Google. https://www.google.com/